CYNTHIA HICKEY

MAUI MACADAMIA MADNESS

CYNTHIA HICKEY

DEDICATION

Thank you to God, my husband, my
Children, and to all you wonderful fans
Who contacted me asking for a fourth
Summer Meadows mystery.
God Bless you all..

1

The plane dropped fifty feet. A woman screamed.

I closed my eyes and gripped Ethan's arm like a pit bull to a steak. I—Summer Meadows, uh, Banning, having been married less than twelve hours, I tended to forget my new last name—did not like to fly. Not one iota. "Whose idea was it to fly to Maui?"

Ethan laughed and pulled me as close as the armrest between us would allow. "Yours. I wanted to cruise, but you said you didn't want to leave Aunt Eunice with the store for too long."

"You should have stopped me. I was delusional." I buried my face in his shirt front. "Out of my mind with marital bliss." My stomach leaped as the plane jumped again. Please, don't let me lose my dinner. Why couldn't the airline have a direct flight to Maui instead of their having to fly a prop plane from the main island to their destination?

Ethan rubbed my head. "Did you manage to sleep? I'd hate for you to arrive in Maui with gritty eyes."

"A little. You?" I peeked up at him, wanting to run my fingers through his mussed hair. One night as his wife, and I loved him even more than before.

"Like a baby."

I'd hardly slept a wink. Something about there

being nothing but air between me and the ocean kept me awake and white knuckled. Not to mention the man behind us who snored like a bulldog with sinus problems. "I'll sleep once we reach the Bed and Breakfast in Kihei." I grinned. "But hopefully not too much."

Ethan bent and gave me one of his heart-stopping, lip-searing kisses. Normally, people might think getting married on April Fool's Day a bad omen, but not me. I thought it funny and unique. Just like me and my new husband. Doing things out of the ordinary kept life interesting.

I loosened my grip on his arm and grabbed the arm rests as the plane began its descent. Fun with the most handsome man on God's green earth, no dead bodies or internet scams, no one shooting at me, all pointed to the most perfect ten days a woman could hope to have.

The plane landed smoothly. Passengers stood and reached for their carry-on bags before the fasten seatbelt light blinked off. I stepped aside and let Ethan handle ours while I tried to peer around people and out the windows. From what I could see, the airport looked like any other one I had been in. A squat white building on a tarmac. I sighed and took my makeup bag. Ethan placed his free hand on the curve of my lower back, sending delicious tremors up my spine, and steered me off the plane.

We made our way to baggage claim, waited until our suitcases arrived, then headed outside to the van that would take us to Wahine's Bed and Breakfast. Lovely young women, arms loaded with leis, welcomed us with "Aloha." The fragrant scent of flowers and ocean filled the air. I breathed deep, certain I was as close to heaven as a woman could get and still be on earth.

Excitement rose like champagne bubbles and colored the day rosy. I fairly skipped to the transport van and showed the driver our registration papers while Ethan lugged the bags. Strong as he was, he groaned under the weight. I tended to over pack, as evidenced by the extra fees for the luggage weight and extra bags. But, a girl had to be prepared for anything.

Three other couples joined us on the van ride, two obviously married, and one that ignored each other. Either they were a couple angry with each other or strangers. Maybe the beauty and romance of Maui would soothe whatever ailed them.

As the driver moved to close the door, another man ran up, shouting for us to wait. The driver scowled and motioned for the man to sit in the front passenger seat. Once everyone and their bags were secure, he slid behind the wheel.

"This is it." I glanced at Ethan. "We're really here. On our honeymoon. On Maui."

He grinned back and squeezed my hand. "Yes, we are."

"Oooh, honeymooners." A plump woman sitting in front of us beamed over the back of the seat. Her greying brown hair was clipped back in flower barrettes and the colors on her tent-of-a-housedress would blind a man with no eyes. "I'm Sharon Aldrich, this is my husband, Ron. We're celebrating our twenty-fifth wedding anniversary. We spent our honeymoon here, too."

Her husband, a round, balding man, nodded and unfolded a newspaper. Sharon tapped the other couple. "Since we're all going to be spending the next few days together, we should get acquainted."

The other couple looked to be in their mid-twenties. "We're Bruce and Maryann Franklin," the young man said. "On our honeymoon." He landed a loud smack on his wife's lips. She reddened and cupped his face. They rubbed noses like a couple of Eskimos.

Sharon turned to the last two. "And you two are?"

"Not married and strangers." The woman pulled a lipstick and compact from her purse. She reminded me of Ethan's ex-girlfriend, Terry Lee. Dark hair, shapely figure, legs that went on forever. I disliked her on the spot. "I'm Susan Wood, here on vacation."

"I'm David Hatcher. Business." He was good looking in a California surfer kind-of-way with longish sun-bleached brown hair and brown eyes. His gaze flicked over Susan's shoulder and landed, for a moment, on the back of the front passenger's head.

"And you, sir?" Sharon leaned forward, trying to gain the attention of the man in front.

"Here on business." He continued to stare out the window. A gold Rolex watch winked from his left wrist.

"Do you know each other?" Sharon motioned between the man and David. When David shook his head and the other man didn't reply, she shrugged and turned back to Ethan and me. "The other honeymooners?"

"Summer and Ethan Banning." I reached out my hand to shake hers. "From Arkansas."

"Well, well," Susan simpered. "So am I. I thought you looked familiar. You're the wannabe sleuth from Mountain Springs. I read about you in the Arkansas

River News."

"Nothing wannabe about it." I lifted my chin. "I solved three crimes." And almost died solving each one of them.

Ethan placed a restraining hand on my leg and leaned close. "We're on our honeymoon, Tinkerbell. No crime talk."

I got the warm fuzzies at the nickname he used to tease me with because of my petite size. What a turnaround from when I used to take offense. I felt the love in his words. I patted his leg. "I know." I transferred my attention to the lush greenery passing outside the window.

Wahine's Bed and Breakfast sat on a private beach, its pristine white siding a brilliant contrast to the azure sky. Off to the sides sat quaint huts with thatched roofs and cascading blossoms dripping from the eaves. Opposite the hotel, the beach sparkled like diamonds, inviting a person to indulge in an oceanic dip. I couldn't wait to sink my toes into the wet sand at the water's edge.

"Aloha!" A brown-skinned couple, him in a tropical shirt and her in a purple muumuu, held their arms wide in welcome. "Your home awaits you," the man said. "I am Larry Wahine, and this is my princess-of-a-bride, Anna."

How sweet of him to call his wife his princess. I glanced up at Ethan, who grinned and planted a kiss on my nose.

"You've been my princess from the moment I first laid eyes on you when you were a skinny, freckle-faced, twelve-year-old."

He always knew exactly what to say to heat up the water.

"We have lots of fun planned," Mr. Wahine explained. "From snorkeling to luaus, parasailing to whale watching. We hope that all of you will join in the group activities, but if not," his smile never faded. "We will guide you where you want to go. Now, to show you to your rooms. Come, follow me."

"I hope you paid attention to my reservation requests," Mr. Businessman said. "I requested a cottage set apart from the others."

"Yes, Mr. Jamison, we've set you aside as far as possible." I wasn't sure, but I would have sworn Mr. Wahine actually rolled his eyes.

"This way, Mr. and Mrs. Banning." Mrs. Wahine headed left, motioning for the other honeymooners to follow us. "Our honeymoon cottages are this way. It allows for a little more privacy." She winked and opened the door to our suite. "We do rent a few rooms in the main house, but folks tend to enjoy it out here more."

Wicker furniture and tropical fabrics welcomed us. A large basket of fruit with a platter of cheese and bread beside it sat on a coffee table. Although this was our second night as husband and wife, my face burned at sight of the king-sized bed draped with mosquito netting.

Ethan sat our bags beside the bed then moved to open the French doors. "Look at this view, Summer."

I slipped under his arm and took in the scene in front of me. Waves caressed the beach, palm trees swayed, and the last of the day's wind surfers filled the ocean with bright colors. "Paradise."

He squeezed me. "Do you want to eat in tonight, or join the others?"

"I'd like to eat right there from the fruit basket." I

motioned at the small bistro table on our deck. "Do you think the Wahine's will mind?"

"I'm sure they expect it from newlyweds."

"Most likely."

"Sit while I get the basket." He moved inside. "There's a bottle of sparkling cider and one of grape juice. Which do you want?"

"The cider, please." I sat in a wicker chair and the fuschia cushions let out a *whoosh*. I set my feet on the small footstool in front of me. I could sit there every night and watch the sun go down past the water.

Especially if Ethan sat beside me. He placed the basket and tray on a wrought iron patio table, then went back inside for our drinks, leaving me to cut the bread with the knife provided.

"Look, Ethan, a box of chocolate-covered macadamia's." I lifted a white box wrapped with a sunshine yellow ribbon from the basket. I had started serving them in my store, but the nuts had a tendency to spoil so quickly, I didn't stock them as often as I would like. This was a rare treat. I opened the box, picked out a couple of pieces, and settled back to enjoy the view.

Did the natives of Hawaii ever get used to the sight of a crimson sun lowering over water painted with magenta and pumpkin, or did they take the sight for granted? I sighed and watched as the last wind surfer strolled across the beach and past the hotel.

"To us." Ethan handed me a wine glass and bent to kiss me.

"To us." I raised my glass in toast, returned his kiss, and then transferred my attention back to the beach.

Someone ran through the deepening shadows.

"Looks like one of the guests is enjoying an early evening jog." I took a sip of my drink as he or she ran past our balcony, a dark-colored hoodie pulled over their head. I shrugged. To each their own, my Aunt Eunice always said.

With the sun setting, the weather cooled off, but not enough to warrant even a light weight jacket, at least in my opinion. The person glanced toward us. Their steps faltered as I raised my glass, then the person sprinted off.

A scream shattered the peace of the night.

2

I jumped to my feet and dashed toward the door.

Ethan shot out a hand to stop me. "Where do you think you're going?"

"To see what happened." A dark figure on the beach. An unearthly scream. What did he expect me to do? Go to bed and forget all about it?

"We're on our honeymoon. We will not get involved." He crossed his arms. Apparently he did expect me to ignore the scream.

"But Ethan, what if—"

"What if nothing." He narrowed his eyes. "I'm not a heavy-handed person, Summer, but I will lay down the law in this case. No." He pointed at my seat. "Please, sit and finish your drink. If it is something we need to be concerned about, Mr. or Mrs. Wahine will let us know."

"You're right." I plopped back in the chair. It's possible I put too much stock in a scream. What if someone was being tickled? Or had cold water dumped on their head? I took a sip of my drink, the apple flavored carbonation sliding over my tongue. I hesitated before swallowing. What if someone was being murdered? I swallowed hard and plunked the glass on the table.

"Let's at least go to the lobby. I won't be able to rest otherwise. You know how I am." I gave Ethan my best puppy dog eyed look.

"Yes, I do. Fine." He held out his hand. "You've got five minutes."

That's all I would need to find out what was happening. I slipped my hand in his and flashed a grin. "You're the best husband ever!"

"Right. You're only happy because I spoil you." He tapped my nose. "Rotten, I might add."

"Because you love me." I kissed him and tugged until we left our cottage.

A soft ocean breeze caressed my face as we passed others who obviously had the same intent we did. A small group of hotel guests converged in the courtyard. Their whispers filled the air with sound as effectively as the cicadas back home. Goosebumps broke out on my arms. Something big happened, I just knew it!

"Well, I heard someone found him dead."

I turned to glimpse a young man in khaki pants and Hawaiian shirt. "Who?"

"Malia, the maid, found Mr. Jamison dead in his bathtub." He shook his head. "A box of nuts scattered across the floor like marbles."

"He was poisoned?" I ate nuts. I clutched my stomach. "Wait. How do you know this?"

"Camilla Wahine told me. She's Anna and Larry's daughter." He looked at me as if I were an idiot.

"I haven't had the pleasure of meeting her." I crossed my arms. "Who are you?"

"Manuel Mokiao, the gardener." He mimicked

me with the arms and leaned closer. "They have a son, too. His name is Leroy. Who are you?"

"I wouldn't tell her a thing, if I were you." Susan Wood sashayed up in a silky nightgown and robe in a melon color that complemented her surroundings. "She fancies herself a detective." She smirked. "Not a very attractive quality in a woman." Her gaze raked over Ethan. I could almost guarantee she purred.

Couldn't she at least get dressed before congregating with the rest of us? "I do not." I didn't 'fancy' myself anything. I was a sleuth and a very good one.

"Settle down." Ethan stepped closer and put his arm around my shoulders. "Don't let her get your goat."

I could *not* believe that a murder occurred on my honeymoon, much less that another beautiful evil temptress wanted me to feel inferior as a woman and looked at Ethan as if he were something to be devoured. "I won't."

More people gathered, and I scanned the crowd for someone wearing a dark-colored hoody. Not to say for sure that that person was responsible, but they were the most suspicious at the moment.

While clothing ranged from nightclothes to bathing suits to tropical wear, not one person wore sweats and a hooded jacket. Experience had taught me that the suspect always came back to the crime, especially when a crowd gathered. I took mental note of those in attendance.

Manuel, the gardener, all those from the van, a couple of strangers, nobody who stood out as a murderer. Well, I'd been in similar circumstances and still managed to catch the bad guy. Of course, it was usually because my life was in danger, and I got them before they got me, but I had faith that this time, things would be different.

I glanced up at my new husband. Things would be different because I was not going to get involved. Not on my honeymoon.

A young man and woman dressed in the floral uniform of the Bed and Breakfast sidled up next to the gardener. They had to be the prettiest people I had ever seen.

The girl smiled from behind her curtain of silky hair. "Welcome to Maui, I am Camilla Wahine."

I returned her smile, taken back by the fact her welcome didn't quite meet her eyes. "Summer Meadows, I mean Banning. You found the body?"

"Yes. It was horrible." Her shark eyes filled with tears. Maybe I was wrong about her smile feeling forced. Most likely, she really was distraught and forced her smile out of habit. "The police are there now and said I cannot leave here." She clutched the man's hand next to her. "Leroy, do they think I did this?"

"They couldn't." He kept his eyes focused on the doors to the Bed and Breakfast's main building. "Nobody would believe them."

The paramedics wheeled out a body covered with a sheet. Bob Jamison's left arm hung, the hand dangling.

I clutched Ethan's arm. "His watch is gone."

"What?"

"Mr. Jamison is not wearing his Rolex. I noticed it on the bus." I scanned the area for a police officer. "Maybe his death is theft related."

Ethan sighed. "I thought you weren't going to get

involved. He was found in the bathtub, correct?"

"I'm not getting involved, but I do think I should let the authorities know, don't you?" I stood on tip-toe to see over people's heads. At five foot two, most people stood at least a few inches taller than me.

An officer conversed with the Wahine family, notepad in hand, pen busy scratching down notes. He kind of reminded me of a bulldog, the way his forehead hung over his eyes and his heavy jowls lined his mouth. Hopefully, he was a friendly person, unlike my cousin Joe who was an officer back home. Joe actually treated me as a nuisance.

"Officer." My sandals slapped the sidewalk. "Did anyone check for Mr. Jamison's watch?"

"Excuse me?" Officer Manano, his tag read. "Who are you?"

"I'm Summer Banning, one of the guests here. On the bus earlier today, Mr. Jamison—"

"Ma'am, I must insist you step aside and let us do our job." He made a sweeping motion with his arm.

"But, sir, it's possible that—"

He pushed past me and into the main building, leaving me standing with my mouth hanging open and steam coming out of my ears. I couldn't remember the last time I had been treated so rudely.

I stormed back to Ethan and grabbed his hand. "Let's go back to our room. That man wasn't interested in a thing I had to say. I need to call your sister." April, Ethan's younger sister and my best friend, would lend me a sympathetic ear.

"The honeymoon's over already?" Ethan pulled me to his side and kissed the top of my head.

"Of course not, silly, but if I don't talk to someone, I'll burst."

"I'm someone."

I was a dunce. Of course, he was. My blond, blue eyed, Adonis. "You're the best someone. So, tell me, hot stuff, why wouldn't the officer spare me a moment to hear what I had to say?" I stopped and planted fists on my hips.

"He's busy?" Ethan leaned against a railing. "It's very possible the watch is sitting on Bob Jamison's dresser."

"And it's equally possible it isn't." I marched away and through the door of our cottage. The Rolex could be nestled in someone's pocket waiting to be sold. A piece of jewelry worth thousands was definitely a motive for murder.

My stomach rumbled, reminding me I'd had very little to eat since our plane landed. I headed for the patio and the basket of fruit and cheese. This is where the latest mystery would begin. I settled into the wicker lounge chair.

"Somebody, the killer, maybe, jogged down the beach. Then, I heard a scream, most likely from Camilla, since she found the body. Of course, this is only what I saw and heard. I could be totally off track and grasping at straws." I pulled a few grapes off a cluster. Ethan was still inside, but I tended to talk out loud when working through a problem, so I'd catch him up when he joined me. My hand paused on the way to my mouth. "What if he died of natural causes?"

"Exactly." Ethan handed me a blended pineapple drink. "Virgin Pina Colada. Just because nuts were on the bathroom floor, doesn't mean there was poison involved. He could have had a heart attack, choked, any number of things."

"But what if there was foul play?" I took a sip. Pineapple, coconut, and citrus flavors burst on my tongue. "Oh, yum!"

"You're always looking for a mystery to solve."

"It's fun." I shrugged. "A year ago, I never would have thought about solving a crime, much less a murder, and now I've solved three."

"And almost died in the process." Ethan pulled his lounge chair closer to mine. "Now that I have you, I don't want to lose you."

"Excuse me." I play-punched his shoulder. "I think I did the chasing. You didn't think of me as anything but April's pesky friend for years!"

He laid his hand on my thigh and grinned. "I don't think of you as that anymore."

I leaned forward for a kiss.

A spear whipped past me and imbedded into the cottage wall.

3

Ethan grabbed me around the shoulders and took me and the deck chair to the wood planks of the patio floor. His elbow slammed into my breasts and drove the air from me in a rush of pain. I hung over the arm of the chair, rear in the air, and prayed another spear didn't catch me in the behind.

"Are you all right?" Ethan tugged at me until I lay flat next to him, my heart racing, and me gasping, trying to put together what had happened.

"Did somebody actually throw a spear at us?" I craned my neck.

Sure enough, a spear held a piece of paper to the side of our cottage. "A note." I pushed to my feet and ripped the message free. "Go home."

I handed the note to Ethan and peered into the night. A person would have had to have been close in order to throw something as archaic as a spear. I leaned over the railing and searched both ways. "There's nobody here."

"Get down!" Ethan grabbed the hem of my dress and tugged me back next to him. "We need to let the

Wahine's know. Good grief. We haven't been here twenty-four hours, and you've managed to get us neck deep into trouble."

I plopped next to him, my floral skirt ballooning around me. "We aren't going home, are we?"

"No, we aren't." Ethan took my hand and we crawled into the room. "And we aren't going to skip the fun things on our list, either."

"Can we try to find out what happened to Mr. Jamison?" *Please, please, please.*

He tapped my nose. "We'll leave that up to the police."

"But what if we get another threat?" I stood and pulled the curtains closed.

"We'll discuss that if it happens." Ethan picked up the phone, asked the Wahine's to call the police, then dropped onto the sofa. "Let's cuddle until the cops get here."

As hot as he was, snuggling was the last thing on my mind after someone tried to kill us. Nevertheless, we were on our honeymoon, and a few kisses would get me in the mood fast enough. I closed my eyes and puckered up. After a couple seconds of … nothing, I opened them. "What?"

"You aren't in it."

"Yes, I am."

He shook his head. "What's going through that pretty red head of yours?"

"My hair is auburn, thank you. Doesn't it concern you that one of us could have been killed?"

"Yes." He rolled his shoulders. "I really did pray that we could have an uneventful ten days on Maui. I see now that no time with you will ever be uneventful. What do you want to do?"

Hope bubbled up in me like the effervescent bubbles in the sparkling cider I had drunk. "Ask a few questions? Find out whether Mr. Jamison died naturally or by evil intent." I kissed the end of his nose. "How many people get to solve a crime in the beauty of Hawaii?"

"Seeing as how someone wants us gone, I believe there *is* something to discover now."

A knock pounded on the door.

Ethan stood. "We'll come up with a plan after the cops leave." He flashed a smile. "I might actually enjoy being your sidekick for once, instead of the person telling you to stay out of things." He strolled to the door.

I couldn't wait to phone April and tell her what I'd landed in this time! Don't get me wrong, I still intended to witness all the wonders of the island while solving Mr. Jamison's murder. I was on my honeymoon, after all.

Officer Manano, and a younger African American policeman I hadn't seen before, bustled into the living area of the cottage. Officer Manano gave me a stern look, which I returned with a glare of my own. "Where's the spear?"

I motioned my head toward the patio then leaped from the sofa. "I tried to tell you that I have experience—"

He looked past me to Ethan. "You said there was a note?"

"Yes, sir." Ethan handed him the ripped sheet of notebook paper.

"Hmmm." Officer Manano handed it to his partner, who tucked it into a paper bag. "Are you leaving? I suggest you don't."

"Why?" I rushed to his side. "Are we suspects? Someone threw a spear at us!"

"You are persons of interest, yes." His brown face remained emotionless. "All the guests here are. I've heard of you, Mrs. Banning. You and your need to poke into police business. My suggestion is for you to enjoy your honeymoon and let the authorities handle this."

I crossed my arms. "How did you hear about me?" I was going to bash Susan Wood's teeth in if she was spreading malicious gossip about me to the police. Why had that woman taken such a dislike to me? We had never met before the shuttle bus ride.

Officer Manano chose not to answer. He turned to Ethan. "Will you be staying here for the duration of your stay?"

Ethan nodded, his brows drawing to a V. Good. He wasn't happy about being a suspect any more than I was.

"What do you do for a living, Mr. Banning?" Officer Manano nodded to his partner.

I could see his badge now, Officer Williams. He poised his pen over his paper.

"I'm a high school woodshop teacher." Ethan crossed his arms, giving me a delightful view of his own 'guns'. "My wife owns Summer Confections, a candy store in Mountain Springs, Arkansas. We are on our honeymoon. We were married yesterday. Why, exactly, do you have us as persons of interest? We didn't know Mr. Jamison before this afternoon. We aren't the sort of people to poison someone's macadamia nuts."

Poor thing. Unfortunately, Ethan knew the drill when questioned by officers of the law. Something he could pin on me because of my past escapades. Only thing was, this time he wasn't being questioned by a friendly face.

Officer Manano narrowed his eyes. "Who said anything about poisoned nuts?"

"So, it is true." I popped a grape into my mouth. "I figured as much."

"Mrs. Banning." High spots of color appeared on Manano's cheeks. "If you don't stay out of my investigation, then I'll be going with the assumption that you planted those poisoned nuts in an insane attempt for more notoriety in solving crimes and to get your face plastered in the Maui newspaper."

Not many things leave me speechless, but that comment did. Tears burned the back of my eyelids. How could a complete stranger be so cruel? I hated having my picture taken.

Ethan marched to the door. "I must insist that unless you have a warrant, it is time for the two of you to leave."

"Stick around, Mr. Banning. We'll be in touch." Officer Manano strode through the door.

Officer Williams stepped onto the back porch, retrieved an awesomely carved wooden spear with a shark's tooth spearhead, then followed his senior partner.

By the time Officer Friendly and Officer No Speech left, my stomach was growling in earnest. I didn't think a few chunks of cheese and some grapes would do the trick. "I'm starving."

Ethan cast a wide-eyed gaze on me. "How can you eat at a time like this? That man thinks we killed someone just so you could get your name and face in another newspaper."

I shrugged. "I'm used to people thinking the worst. We'll prove him wrong." I slid my arms around his waist and laid my cheek on his chest. His heart raced. Maybe I could skip food in favor of something more delicious. I peered up at him. "Wanna go to bed?"

###

"I could not believe the nerve of that man. He really hurt my feelings." I scooted higher on the headboard and stared through the bedroom door. Ethan would be home any moment with our breakfast.

"How do you manage to get into these predicaments?" April sighed through the phone. "Joe is going to throw a gasket when he hears."

"You should have seen Ethan. I don't think I've ever seen him so angry." A breeze blew through the open window and fluttered the white gauzy curtains. The sun rose above the azure sea, calling for vacationers to don swimsuits and snorkel gear. I couldn't wait to get my feet wet. As long as I didn't meet the shark whose tooth was recently in our cottage wall.

"Since you're knee deep in another mystery, are you going to try and solve it?"

"Of course. You know me." My fingers itched to take up pen and paper and start taking notes.

"Yes, I do. Please, be careful. On a better subject, how's the honeymoon?"

"Wonderful." I snuggled into the pillows. "I married the best man in the world."

"Actually, I think Joe is."

"Of course you aren't going to think your brother is the best. How are your wedding plans coming along?" The front door clicked closed and the enticing aroma of coffee made its way to the bedroom.

"Great. Right on schedule. And don't say anything else about how a June wedding is cliché, I know it is, but that's what I've always wanted."

"I'm happy for you. Ethan is back with food. I'd better go. I'll keep you informed. Bye." I clicked off, slid the phone onto the nightstand, and greeted Ethan with a smile. "Hey, baby."

"Still hungry?" He set a tray of fruit and pastries on the bed then plopped next to me.

"Starving!" I grabbed a cream cheese Danish. If I didn't start eating something of substance, all the carbs were going to make my behind as big as the island. "What's on the agenda today?"

"Do you want to snorkel right off the beach here or go up to the resort?"

"Since I've never snorkeled, I'd like to try here first." The pastry melted in my mouth with cheesy creaminess. I reached for another. By sticking around the B & B, I might find an opportunity to question someone, anyone, seeing as how I had absolutely no suspects at this point. Except for Susan Wood. She's the only person here who knew who I was and who could have told Officer Friendly I was in the paper back home.

Someone knocked on the door. When Ethan moved to answer, I ducked into the bathroom. I might as well get dressed. I had bought a new red bikini with white polka dots and a sheer gauzy white scarf to tie around my hips. I couldn't wait to dazzle Ethan. Once dressed, I slipped my feet into sandals which sported a big red flower on them, and stepped into the living room.

I smiled as Ethan's eyes widened in appreciation. Mr. Wahine grinned beside him. Yep, I still had appeal.

Ethan strolled up to me, the sparkle in his eyes never fading, and swiped a finger across my chest. "Were you saving that blob of cream cheese for later?"

"Yes." My shoulders slumped. So much for a sexy entrance. "Good morning, Mr. Wahine."

"Aloha, Mrs. Banning. I came to see how you were after last night's fright."

"All in the past." I sat on the sofa, crossed my legs, and tried to look as alluring as possible in order to remove the mental picture of me with food on my bosom from Ethan. Although I was built petite, God saw fit to amply endow me, and they tended to catch 'things' such as food. By the age of thirty, I should know better than to step outside the bathroom without checking.

"We would like to give you free tickets to a luau on Friday night for your misfortune." He handed them to Ethan. "My son and daughter will be dancing."

"Thank you so much!" I clapped my hands. I've always wanted to see men in grass skirts play with fire.

Now might be a good opportunity for the first of my questions. I avoided Ethan's gaze so he couldn't send me signals to stop. "How are the other guests faring after Mr. Jamison's death, and now this?"

Mr. Wahine shook his head. "As well as can be expected. My poor daughter is the most traumatized. My son seems to be angry that this has happened, as it will not look favorably on the hotel. The other guests are looking at it as excitement for their vacation." His grin returned. "We just booked our two-bedroom cottage. The party arrives in the morning. This may help our business. You know what they say, any advertising is good advertising." He tossed us a wave and backed out of the room.

Hmmm. I chewed my pinkie nail. Was the Wahine Bed and Breakfast in financial trouble? What sort of business did Mr. Jamison do? I glanced out the window to see Susan Wood in a black string bikini head for the beach.

"Ready?" I popped up from the sofa, grabbed a waterproof bag that held towels, sun screen, and the latest mystery from James Patterson.

Ethan cocked his head. "What are you up to? What questions could you possibly have to ask Susan?"

"I won't know until we start talking." I kissed him and skipped out the door.

Ethan followed with the snorkel gear. "I may soon regret saying you could try solving this." He closed the door and locked it behind us.

The Aldrichs came out of their cabin and headed for the beach. Wonderful. Sharon was much more communicative than Susan.

Ethan put his arm around my shoulders. "Before you start bugging people, you have to go snorkeling with me first. Don't forget why we're on Maui."

"I wouldn't dream of it." I slipped my hand in his and let him lead me to a stretch of sand a little away from the others.

Off the shore, a small reef formed an almost complete circle. The area looked safe enough for me.

It wasn't big enough for man-eating sharks. I kicked off my shoes and slipped on the flipper fins. Once I managed to get that mouth breathing apparatus over my head without the rubber band pulling all my hair out, I slapped my way into the delicious water. Ah, I could stay out there all day.

After a few minutes of getting up enough nerve to let my feet come out from under me and to lay face first in the water, I opened my eyes and surveyed the murky world around me. I thought the water in Hawaii was clear?

My face mask fogged up. I pushed my feet back to the silty ocean floor. After removing the mask, I spit in it as I had seen divers on television do, then slapped around until I was once again laying on my face in the water. Someone tapped me on the head.

Didn't they know how long it took me to get in that position?

Ethan stared at me. "Stop mixing up the bottom. You're making the water murky. Just fall forward or squat then let your feet up."

Oh. That explains the unclear view down below. "Thanks, sweetie."

I tried again and succeeded. Once the water cleared, I spotted all types of marine life. Deciding to follow the reef, I skimmed along the top, spotting black and yellow striped fish with fins, some silver sparkly ones, and one that looked like a snake. I steered clear of that one. The sun's rays warmed my shoulders and the top of my head. I couldn't think of a more pleasant way to spend a Saturday morning.

A lot of people thought us strange to get married when we did, but we were set on April Fools and couldn't wait until the day fell on a weekend. I struck an underwater pose.

Ethan took a picture of me through an underwater camera then swam in the opposite direction. I turned back to study the reef. An eel poked its head from a hole and came straight for me. I gurgled like an actress in an underwater B-horror movie and backpedaled as fast as I could. Didn't eels bite? I wished I would have read the pamphlet that came with our snorkeling gear. Gasping for breath, I stood and pulled off my mask.

Leroy Wahine stood on the reef grinning. "Aloha."

"I was attacked by an eel."

His smile never faded. "Are you enjoying the fish? This small reef circle is a nursery. You can see the same species much larger by the resort. Molokini is where you want to worry about getting bit."

A baby eel? My face heated, and it wasn't from the sun. "It's fantastic." Lifting my feet as high as possible so I didn't stir up the ocean floor, I plopped my way to shore.

Good grief! Susan Wood lay on her stomach, bathing suit top untied, and talked to David Hatcher. I immediately scoped the area for Ethan, relieved to see him still snorkeling.

I tossed my gear to the sand and plopped on my beach towel. Might as well try to get some sun on my mayonnaise-white legs. Maybe I would overhear some tidbit of titillating conversation between Susan and David. I put on my mirrored sunglasses and floppy hat and did my best to be inconspicuous.

"I met with him last night, and he didn't say a thing about anyone being a suspect." Susan twirled a paper umbrella in a mango-colored drink.

"Obviously," David dug his toes into the sand. "He doesn't tell you everything."

"He should, if he knows what's good for him." Susan cut me a sideways glance. "But enough of that with Nosey Nellie sitting here. How are you, Summer?"

"Wonderful." I kept my gaze trained on Ethan, who laughed at something Leroy said. Dripping water, hair slicked back, and blue swim trunks that matched the ocean, I don't think I had ever seen anything that looked better. Including the scenery.

"Heard someone threw a stick at you." Susan giggled along with David's chuckle.

This time I did look at her. "What is your problem? You've been on my case since yesterday. Unless I'm mistaken, we've never met. If I have managed to wrong you somehow, please accept my apology." I stood, shook off my towel, deriving a small bit of pleasure at the sand that rained over her shiny, oiled skin, and marched a few yards down the beach. So much for garnering valuable information. Some things were not worth the trouble.

Of course, I would like to know who she had been talking to David about.

4

I smoothed the skirt of the white sundress I wore to show off my glowing sunburn, and sat in the chair Ethan pulled out for me. The menu said we were being served pineapple ham. Although jet lag had caught up with me, I didn't want to pass up what the Wahine's claimed was a traditional Hawaiian meal. Nor did I want to miss another chance to possibly glean clues from the other guests.

The Aldrichs were across from us, the Franklins at the opposite end of the table. Susan, David, Officer Manano, and a couple of other faces I didn't recognize filled the other seats. Several small tables dotted the outskirts of the room if someone desired a more intimate dining experience.

I met Manano's unsmiling gaze with a grin, then turned to Ethan who sat on my right. The one long table didn't provide much opportunity for conversation except for those sitting close. The delectable aromas coming from the kitchen made my mouth water. I decided the food would be worth the lack of information gathering.

I must have had my gumshoeing look on my face, because Ethan squeezed my hand, and whispered for me to be more subtle. I couldn't believe that I was married to the world's most handsome man and that he had agreed to help me solve a mystery. God couldn't have given me a better honeymoon. Romance and a mystery to solve. I was one blessed gal.

"The thrown spear must have been so frightening." Sharon Aldrich stabbed a chunk of pineapple with her fork. "I heard, just a couple of inches to the left, and you would have sported an extra hole in your body."

Amazing how confidential news, such as a police report, traveled so quickly to the other guests. I gave Manano a stern glance. He acted as if he couldn't see me and continued talking to Susan. How was I supposed to find out what happened to Jamison if the local police blabbed to everyone within ear shot? Detective work required secrecy. Stealth. I transferred my attention back to Sharon.

"It was scary. Luckily for me, my new husband has good reflexes." I smiled at Ethan and cut into my ham.

Sharon shook her head. "Almost makes me rethink our decision to spend our anniversary here. I'm not much of one for adventure, and to have a murder and an attempted murder happen in the same night? Well!"

"Now, honey," her husband, Ron, patted her hand. "Crime exists everywhere. Jamison and Mrs. Banning were just in the wrong place at the wrong time. Jamison wasn't very well liked in certain circles, you know."

I paused at putting my fork in my mouth. "I thought you didn't know Jamison." Weren't they the ones who had everyone introduce themselves on the bus?

Ron peered over the rim of his tropical drink. "I've heard things."

"What sort of things?"

Ethan kicked me under the table. "When we've finished dinner, we can take a stroll along the beach. I know you said you wanted to watch the sun rise and set each day."

"I thought you were going to help me." I hissed out the side of my mouth, and then grinned at the couple across the table.

"I am, but behind the scenes."

"That's not a very effective way." I had picked up my glass to prevent people from reading my lips. Everyone knew a detective needed to ask questions. But, Ethan was new to this, so I'd let him slide. This time.

I craned my neck to see what the others were doing. Susan glared at Officer Manano. What was up with that? My senses were tingling. I'd bet a suntan there was more to Susan's coming to Hawaii than just a vacation.

I couldn't allow myself to be distracted. There was no way I could solve two puzzles at once, especially when one was a woman's relationship with a man. Since I didn't care for either of them, it shouldn't be a difficult decision, but my gut told me there was more to the situation than I was seeing. When Susan excused herself from the table and headed to the restroom, I did the same.

Susan bypassed the restroom and disappeared into the room reserved as a library for the guests.

Whispers drifted down the hall.

I slowed my steps, walking as silently as flip-flops would allow and stopped out of sight. Sharon's voice rose in answer to another one. I thought the other voice might belong to the Wahine's daughter, but couldn't make a positive identification. I needed to know before jumping to conclusions.

If I passed the restroom, what excuse could I give? Could I play dumb and pretend to borrow a book, unaware that the room was occupied? Why not? The room wasn't a private one.

I took a deep breath and stepped inside. "Oh, excuse me."

It wasn't the Wahine's daughter, Camilla, but a maid that spoke with Susan. Both were red in the face and jumped apart when I entered.

"Sorry to interrupt." I moved to a shelf of paperbacks. "I'm just looking for a book to read before falling asleep at night."

"On your honeymoon?" Susan simpered. "That doesn't say much for you or your husband, does it?"

"Don't worry about us." I grabbed the first book my hand came into contact with. "We're doing just fine."

"I wonder…" She nodded her head toward the book in my hand. "Bodice rippers don't bode well for the bedroom."

Horror. I had grabbed a trashy romance novel. "We like to act out the scenes." I did not just say that! I clapped a hand over my mouth and fled like the hounds of hell were on my heels.

Susan's cackle followed. Now, I would most likely never know what the two women argued about. Maybe I didn't need to. But if that was the maid assigned to clean Mr. Jamison's room, I would love to speak with her.

I paused in the doorway of the dining room. What was I going to do with the book? If Ethan saw it, I would never hear the end. I sat it on a table in the foyer, smoothed my dress, took a deep breath, and …

"Aunt Eunice?"

5

A grinning Aunt Eunice and Uncle Roy, accompanied by a serious faced Joe and a sheepish April, stood right inside the French-style front door.

From the footsteps behind me, I knew Ethan had joined us. I closed my eyes, took a deep breath, and forced a smile. What in heaven's name was the family doing here on my and Ethan's honeymoon?

Ethan slid his arm around my waist. "What are they doing here?"

"No idea." I shrugged. "I did *not* invite them." I snuck a sideways glance.

Ethan gritted his teeth, his smile forced, and extended his hand. "Roy, Eunice, you two, this is a … surprise."

"Isn't it?" Uncle Roy pumped his hand. "When Summer told April about her latest shenanigans, and April passed the info along to Eunice, why, there wasn't any resting until we had seats booked on the next flight out of Little Rock. I planned on coming out later in the year to check on a possible investment, so decided to kill two birds with one stone, so to speak. I'm bushed."

"I see." Ethan glowered at his sister. "We were

just finishing up supper. I'll let the Wahine's know y'all are here." His arm slid from around me like frigid water.

I could tell when his glance fell on the book on the table. He gave me a raised eyebrow look. I shrugged. What could I say after all? That I panicked in my snooping? If I showed the smallest amount of fear, Ethan would shut my gumshoeing down faster than a downpour ruined a picnic.

"Great." Uncle Roy clapped. "I'm starved." He patted his overall-clad stomach and strode in the direction of the dining room.

"I'm sorry." April sidled up to me. "I had no idea this would happen when I told Aunt Eunice about our conversation. It just slipped out about the murder and the spear."

"Don't worry about it." I kept my smile firmly in place. "Your brother won't stay mad at me once he realizes I didn't plan this."

"Even he couldn't be that silly." April straightened. "What woman wants family on her honeymoon? Joe is pretty livid himself. Says if anyone shows up when we're on our honeymoon, he'll shoot them."

"Are we interfering?" Aunt Eunice's grin faded. "We only want to help. Dying on your honeymoon is the worst thing that could happen to a person."

Well, okay, but I think being murdered at any moment would be pretty horrible. I disentangled myself from my aunt and best friend and went in search of my husband.

Only a few guests sat at the dining table eating dessert. Ethan wasn't one of them. Since I hadn't seen him in the foyer, I headed to the veranda. Sure enough, his handsome profile was traced with a crimson and pumpkin sunset glow. Dancing palm trees rose behind him.

"I'm sorry. I shouldn't have called April, but I had no idea she would tell Aunt Eunice." My heart clogged my throat.

"Come here." Ethan held out his arm, allowing me to slide under. "I know. I'm not angry, just disappointed. I love them dearly, but you know how overbearing your aunt and uncle can be. I don't want to share you right now."

"I feel the same way." I peered up at him. "Do you want to disappear?"

"What do you have in mind?" His teeth flashed.

"A stroll down the beach to somewhere private?"

"You read my mind." He took my hand and, like a couple of teenagers, we dashed down the walk and onto the warm sand.

I resisted the urge to look over my shoulder to see whether we were spotted. My flip-flops slipped off my feet. I left them, enjoying the feel of the cool, wet sand by the water's edge. The fragrance of Plumeria blossoms filled the air.

Ethan pulled me close and tipped my face. In a slow, agonizing motion, he bent to claim my lips. Softly, then with increasing ardor, he left no doubt as to whom I belonged to. Oh, the splendor of a moonlit kiss on a Hawaiian beach. Heaven on earth.

My arms entwined around his neck, and I took his bottom lip between my teeth. Ethan lifted me from my feet and twirled. Giggling, I laid my forehead against his. "I love you."

"Ditto, sweetheart."

I slid down his torso, heat infusing my body with

every inch of contact. Taking him by the hand, I pulled him into a stand of trees. "Let's fool around."

"You are a naughty girl." He plastered me against a tree trunk.

"Oh, yes, I –"

"Summer?" Aunt Eunice's voice rang across the beach.

I clapped a hand over Ethan's mouth. "Shh. If we're quiet, she'll go away."

My aunt's timing was impeccable. I stomped my foot and peered through the night toward the building. I wanted to mess around with my love. Maybe actually pretend Ethan and I *were* in a trashy romance novel. A little hanky-panky in a forbidden location. Just the thought made my face hot. "Do you think we could sneak back to our cottage?"

"No." Ethan's whisper tickled my neck. His nibbles on my earlobe sent delicious tingles down my spine, and my temperature through the clouds. "We'd be spotted for sure."

My breath came in gasps. With each moment, each kiss, each caress, it became imperative that we leave the beach and reach the privacy of our bedroom. Otherwise, I was going to do something totally foolish and wanton.

"Please." I grabbed his hand and looked for an escape route. There. It would require a romp through thick bushes, but we were young. We could do it. "This way."

"As you wish, G.I. Jane." Ethan's chuckle followed as I dragged us through scratchy evergreens.

Freedom was in sight. A sidewalk light illuminated our royal blue door. I took a step.

"I said, nobody can know." Susan's sultry voice

came from our right. "It will ruin me."

Without a word, hardly breathing, I pressed Ethan back out of sight. Holding a finger to my lips, I motioned my head in Susan's direction.

"I don't understand the need for this type of secrecy." A man answered.

Who was that? He sounded familiar, but I couldn't place him. I glanced at Ethan who shrugged.

"It's either my way, Raul, or I'm out." She lowered her voice to a hiss. "People are dying. Not to mention that nosey Summer poking into everyone's business."

"I can take care of her."

I shrank against Ethan. His arms tightened around me.

"How?" Susan asked.

"Don't worry. When I'm finished, everyone around here will think she offed the dead guy to gain attention for herself."

I stiffened. He did not just say that. My fingers curled into fists. I was going to bash both of them!

"Shh." Ethan rested his chin on my head and started walking backward, the way we had come. When we had cleared the brush, he grabbed me by the shoulders. "Don't say a word until we are in our cabin."

I nodded.

He pulled me at a brisk pace to our temporary home. I kept my eyes peeled for family and saw no one. They must have given up the search and retired to their own rooms.

The moment Ethan unlocked our door and pulled me inside, he grabbed me into a hug. "You don't go anywhere alone, do you hear me? How do you get into these situations? You're a trouble magnet, Summer Banning."

I turned my head in order to rescue my smashed nose. "I didn't go looking for trouble, Ethan. I don't know how it always finds me." Much less on my honeymoon. God sure had a sense of humor.

"I don't want anything to happen to you."

I laughed. A nervous habit that I hated at certain times. This being one of them. "I don't either."

He held me out, touching foreheads. "What am I going to do with you?"

"Love me?"

"That, God help me, I do with all my heart." He took both my hands in his and led me to the sofa. "Now, what? You're the expert."

"You helped a lot on the last mystery." And he had. My cheeks heated remembering our make-out sessions while on stakeout. Ethan had given me a birthday party, where all the gifts were tools of the crime solving trade. That, more than anything, had proven his love for me.

"I got locked in a storage shed. You escaped a mad man and rescued me."

"Oh, yeah." I laid my head on his shoulder. "Don't you forget it, either. Guess I'll need to keep you safer this time. I doubt I'll find a group of high school football players to help this time."

No amount of teasing would alleviate the shadow of dread beginning to hover. Too many times I came close to death. A madman obsessed with love for me and his diamonds. A crazy sideshow freak at the county fair. A devious love triangle and computer scam.

I sighed. Here I was again, through no fault of my

own, except for being in the right place at the wrong time. My ears burned, thinking of how strangers could believe I would kill someone in order to garner fame.

"Don't worry." Ethan's arms tightened around me. "We'll take care of this together. You, me, and God."

"Don't forget Aunt Eunice, Uncle Roy, April, and Joe." I giggled.

Ethan's fingers dug into my sides as he tickled me. "How could I forget them? Your aunt ruined a perfectly good moment in the bushes."

I turned to punch his arm. A person in black sweats stood on our patio peering in. I screamed. Ethan jumped to his feet, depositing me on the floor. I scrambled to my feet as he dashed to the door. No way was he leaving me behind.

Ethan stopped at the door and spun to face me. "Call Joe."

"Not Manano?"

"No." His shoulders slumped. "I recognized the voice with Susan. It was Manano's voice."

I gripped his arm. "We tell the police."

"Who are they going to believe? One of their own, or an amateur sleuth out to make a name for herself?" He cupped my cheek. "I'll be right back."

"Please."

He was gone. Vanished in the dark like smoke in a breeze.

With my heart in my throat, I grabbed my cell phone off the coffee table and punched in Joe's number. "Joe."

"Ethan tire of you already?"

"Stop. We had an intruder. Ethan's gone after—"

Click.

Well, being my cousin, it didn't take much for Joe to fill in the blanks. I collapsed on the sofa and waited for one of the men in my life to return. Within minutes, I had dug at my fingernails until one of the beautiful sculpted French tips fell off. So much for pretty hands. I sat on them. Where are Ethan and Joe?

I called April. "Where's my cousin?"

"Isn't he there?"

"I wouldn't be asking you where he was if he was here." My stomach churned. Horror! The bad guy managed to overcome Ethan and Joe. A feat I always thought would be impossible.

"Calm down. I'm sure there's a logical explanation."

"Don't tell me you aren't scared spitless."

"Every time I'm involved in one of your mysteries, I'm terrified."

"Very funny." I glanced at the dark windows. Was the killer watching me? Had he murdered my husband? Tears poured down my cheeks. "Pray, April. I'm losing it over here. I'm not used to being left behind."

"I will. And I'll get Eunice and Roy, too. You know Eunice has a direct line. Even God is afraid of not listening to her."

I laughed through my tears, the sound coming out between a gurgle and a snort. "You're right." Something scraped across the flagstone patio. "I'll talk to you later. Thanks." After hanging up, I grabbed the lamp beside the sofa. Its ceramic base was a better weapon than nothing.

Taking a deep breath, I approached the patio door, holding the lamp like a baseball bat. The shade fell to the floor with a thump, sending ants scurrying down my arms. *Okay, Lord. Here I go. Angels protect me.*

With a trembling hand, I shoved open the door.

Two figures stood there.

I screamed.

6

I punched Ethan in the arm then followed suit with Joe. Afterward, I felt like I had hit a couple of walls. "You scared the wits out of me!" I set the lamp on the nearest table and shook the pain from my hand. "Did you find him?"

"Nope. But we found the clothes." Joe tossed the sweats on the sofa. "No telling if it was a man or a woman?"

"None." Ethan wrapped an arm around my shoulder. "Thank you for doing as I asked and staying put."

"I didn't have a choice. You took off too fast for me to follow." I stretched on tiptoe to kiss his cheek. "Thank you for coming back alive." Taking Ethan's hand and heading for the bedroom, I glanced over my shoulder. "Goodnight, Joe. Thanks for coming."

"Don't you want to talk about the case?" He grinned, although his ears were a bright enough scarlet to light the night. "Should I take these clothes to the police? What about your statement?"

Ethan's steps paused. Poor man. He was clearly torn between wanting to make love to me and keeping me from getting killed by catching a murderer. "Keep the clothes," he said. "And don't bother going to the police. They won't help anyway."

"We'll talk about this tomorrow." I pulled Ethan inside the room and closed the door.

Having upgraded the rental car to a van, our group gathered around Ethan who held a map of the island. I didn't mind sightseeing with the family, but I did insist they follow the schedule Ethan and I had planned. Today, we were off to the whaling town of Lahaina. I couldn't wait to browse the art galleries. I already had my camera slung over my shoulder, comfortable sandals on my feet, and a bright yellow sundress on my body.

"Time to go. I want to get some snorkeling in when we return this afternoon." Maybe the little fishes had grown since yesterday.

"I want to see the whales," Uncle Roy said.

"You see one every time I put on a bathing suit." Aunt Eunice cackled and winked.

"A mythical creature is what I see." He nuzzled her neck. "A siren of the ocean waves."

I sighed. Having grown up with daily doses of witnessing their affection for each other, the physical contact no longer made me want to gag. If they still acted that way while on the downside of sixty, more power to them, but I wished they'd snuggle behind closed doors.

"More like a troll." Aunt Eunice giggled.

"Okay, that's enough." I threw open the van door. "Time to hit the road and stop with the mushiness." Any kissing and snuggling going on would be between me and Ethan.

"But this is like a second honeymoon for us."

Aunt Eunice grunted as she practically crawled into the vehicle.

My gaze met Ethan's over the hood. He grinned and winked. "That's us in thirty years."

I hoped so. Having waited most of my life for Ethan to notice me, I wanted to spend the rest of it beside him. Joe squeezed into the front passenger seat, leaving me to slide in the far back beside April.

"More leg room," he said.

Totally not fair that I wasn't sitting next to my new husband. What if I died on this trip and this was the last time I got to sit next to him? Yes, a bit dramatic, but my brain did tend to venture off in strange directions when threatened with danger.

As Ethan drove, with Joe navigating, I took the time to drink in the scene outside the van window. I wanted to see all Maui had to offer before we headed home.

On the passenger side of the van, lush greenness rose, hugging us with tropical beauty. On the driver's side, a steep cliff fell to an ocean lapping a boulder-strewn shore interspersed with pristine beaches. There didn't seem to be any worry about the beauty disappearing. Not even a mountain goat could make it down there.

No matter where I looked, the scenery calmed, inspired, and coaxed me to stay and rest a while. Maybe I shouldn't have planned each moment of our stay to include sightseeing or a thrill. I probably should have planned time to sit on the beach, Ethan beside me, and let the water lap my legs. Other than watching the sunset each night, I had us on the go from breakfast on.

"Are you still mad we're here?" April leaned to

speak soft enough the others wouldn't hear.

"No. Especially now that Joe can help Ethan find out why someone wants to frame me." Or at least has threatened to. "It isn't like y'all are sharing a cottage."

"Aunt Eunice wanted to suggest you check out of your room, and we all get one large cabin. Joe put a stop to that idea right off the bat."

"Remind me to thank him." I caught Joe's glance through the mirror in his visor. My parents died when I was five, cousin Joe was the closest thing I had to a sibling, and he fit the role of older brother very well. He was bossy and kept an eye on me. I thanked God for him every day, even when I grumbled about Joe's heavy handed ways.

The van pulled as far to the side of the road as possible, and Ethan cut the ignition. "There's a small waterfall, if y'all want to take pictures."

Did I? I wanted to snap a memory of every second. I practically crawled over April and Aunt Eunice in my excitement.

Ethan's waterfall was more like a trickle over moss-covered rocks on a hillside, but I took the picture anyway. A trickle on Maui is different than a trickle in Arkansas. More romantic for one. I grinned at Ethan.

The sun highlighted his hair with gold. It really wasn't fair how a few days in the sun gave his dark blond hair highlights that cost a pretty fortune for someone at a salon. My own hair would sport brassy red streaks by the end of our Hawaiian stay.

"All y'all stand against that greenery. It will make a gorgeous picture!" I hadn't planned on others being in our honeymoon snapshots, but it couldn't be helped now, so I'd make the best of things.

"Let me take one of you and Ethan first." April took the camera. "After all, we're the ones imposing."

True. I grabbed Ethan's hand and dragged him to stand in front of our 'waterfall'. I had a feeling that we would see real falls of water within a day or two. Rip-roaring, cascading streams that thundered to a crystal pool a hundred feet below.

Once April finished, we took turns taking shots of each couple. I aimed the camera at Aunt Eunice and Uncle Roy, then backed as far across the road as I felt safe. I had no desire to topple over the cliff.

"Say Hawaii is heaven." I lifted the camera to my eye.

A breeze sprang up, teasing the hem of my dress and flirting with my hair. If I could fly, I'd take that two more steps and sail off into Hawaii's heavenly sky.

"Summer, freeze!" Ethan leaped out of the road and in my direction.

I caught my breath, afraid to move. Kind of like the time an African lion snuck up behind me. I learned very quickly to listen when Ethan gave the order not to move.

A silver Nissan Maxima with dark tinted windows sped past us on the narrow road. There was barely room for one vehicle, much less two. Definitely no room for a pedestrian on the side of the road.

I gasped, hugged the camera to my chest, and fought to keep my feet from slipping on the loose gravel. I glanced over my shoulder to the turquoise ocean far below. The world spun. Spots swam before my eyes. I tottered. I couldn't breathe.

Somebody screamed. Maybe either me or April. Maybe both. I slid farther and closed my eyes.

Ethan grabbed my hand and slammed me against his chest, taking us both down hard to the warm asphalt road. "This is beginning to be a habit."

"Not funny." I opened my eyes. "Did that car deliberately try to run over me?"

"I'm sure they were just in a hurry," Uncle Roy said, lifting me off Ethan. "Right, Joe?"

"Yeah, that's it." Joe stared in the direction the Nissan had sped. "There's nobody on earth that wants to do away with Summer. Now or in the past."

"That's enough." Ethan swatted dirt from his backside, gave me a quick kiss, and then stepped over to whisper something to Joe. Soon, the two were deep in a secret conversation. After a few seconds, Uncle Roy joined them. My own little security detail.

I didn't need to be a genius to know I was the topic of their conversation *and* the target of the speeder. Why couldn't I just have an enjoyable honeymoon? Why does somebody always die when I was around?

Slumping against the car, I allowed Aunt Eunice and April to fuss over me. After all, I almost fell to my death.

"That was very frightening." Aunt Eunice smoothed my hair from my face. "Are you all right?"

"I'm fine." I glanced to where the men talked. Why couldn't it be Ethan comforting me? "Just feeling sorry for myself."

"As you should." April crossed her arms and leaned against the car with me. "Wonder what my buffoon of a brother and future husband are cooking up now."

"That buffoon is my husband, and I'm asking you to treat him as such." My mouth quirked.

"As a buffoon or as your husband?" April giggled and hugged me. "I'm so glad we're sisters now."

"Even if being around me might get you killed?"

"Even then." She bumped me with her hip. "Besides, whoever was in that car was after you, not me."

"So you noticed it, too." Obviously Ethan and Joe thought the same thing. So, what were the two cooking up? Occasionally, Uncle Roy would glance over his shoulder like a naughty boy telling a secret. "I think I'm going to ask Ethan for a second honeymoon. This one isn't what I had planned."

Aunt Eunice laughed and playfully slapped my arm. "This one isn't over yet, and you can guarantee this is one you won't forget anytime soon."

I most likely wouldn't forget even without a murder and someone trying to frame me. A girl's honeymoon was like her wedding. Unforgettable. Or should be, even without drama and intrigue. I squared my shoulders. "Let's get moving. Who knows? Maybe we'll run into the Nissan in Lahaina." I hoped so. I'd like to find out who the speeder was and maybe push *them* over a cliff.

Ethan tossed me a thin-lipped smile and climbed behind the wheel of the van. Joe squeezed past me on the middle seat and motioned for me to sit beside him. I rolled my eyes and shook my head.

"I insist." He tipped his head and patted the seat.

Uncle Roy climbed in next, sandwiching me between them, and leaving the far backseat for April and Aunt Eunice. I gave thanks for a day of mild weather and hopefully very little perspiring. Neither Uncle Roy or Joe were small men. I sat with my elbows pressed into my sides and fumed. In that position, I couldn't take pictures of the scenery.

"Scrunch over!" I jabbed Joe.

"There's no room." He shoved back.

"Uncle Roy, sit in the back. There's more space." I crossed my arms. Finding that position no more comfortable, I exhaled and let my hands drop to my lap.

"No, little girl, I'm fine right where I am." He succeeded in crossing his arms, taking up more room, putting his elbow in close contact with my nose.

Mercy! It was going to be a long vacation.

7

We drove by the cutest church. White weathered paneling on the outside. Bright red double doors, shadowed by two massive palm trees. Organ music drifted from the open door and windows. So engrossed was I in the sight and sound of worship in paradise, that we had passed before I opened my mouth to suggest we attend a service. We did have plans to walk through the gardens of a Buddhist temple, though, only because I've never been in one, and curiosity won out.

Out the van window to my left, I made out the sails of a whaling ship. "Find a place to park."

"I will." Ethan steered them into a gravel parking area. "I'm aware of your list of sights to see."

"I don't want to go on the vessel, if we can't sail," I said, climbing out after Uncle Roy. "But I would love to get a couple of photos. I'm more interested in the art galleries."

Uncle Roy groaned, eliciting a glare from me. "What's wrong? You don't have to go. I'm sure you and Aunt Eunice have things you'd rather see."

He connected gazes with Joe, then turned to Ethan. "That all right with you? I think Eunice wants to hit up some Hawaii yard sales."

"Flea market," Aunt Eunice corrected.

"Joe?" Ethan raised his eyebrows.

"We'll go with you." He sighed.

April and I frowned at each other. I shrugged. There was no way of knowing what went through the minds of the men in my family. I wasn't sure I wanted to know. With Ethan on my right, April on my left and Joe next to her, we set off down the sidewalk squashed together like too many people on a bus.

I expelled my breath with enough force to blow my bangs. "Joe, you and April walk behind us. This is ridiculous. One false step and Ethan is in the street."

"Well, I, uh…" He cocked his head in Ethan's direction as if to ask 'what now?'.

Seriously? "You men are protecting me? You think that by having one of you on each side of me each second of the day will keep me safe?" Good grief. "I'm not going to let an idle threat, or a maniac speeding down a road, ruin my honeymoon." I grabbed April's hand. "Come on. The men can walk together."

"Summer." Ethan took my other hand. "We care about you."

"I understand that." Tears stung my eyes. "I have never, nor will I ever, allow some sick minded fool to dictate my life. I did not ask to solve this murder—"

"Yet, you're smack dab in the middle of it," April said. "So, let's solve it. All of us. There's nothing from stopping us from sightseeing and having fun at the same time. Look!" She pointed at an outdoor café. "There are some of the hotel's guests, and it's lunchtime anyway."

Susan Wood and David Hatcher sat cozy at a bistro-style table under a sun-shine yellow umbrella. Instead of sitting across from each other, they sat with shoulders touching and heads bent. At a different table sat the Wahine siblings, along with who I thought might be the maid, Malia. All of a sudden, I found myself very hungry. "I agree. Time to eat."

I led my entourage to the table between the others, smiled at everyone, then hid behind a laminated menu. Maybe, if they thought I was engrossed in ordering, someone might divulge some useful information.

Ethan leaned close. "Maybe if we make out, they won't think we're listening."

Mercy! I grinned. "Not in public, dear husband." One look from his stormy eyes always melted my insides. If I hadn't been raised better, making out in public might have a certain wild allure to it.

"It's always worth a try." He straightened. "You might as well order. I doubt you'll be able to hear anything. Those two seem to be intent on whispering." He nodded at Susan and David.

With April and Joe laughing, the waiters taking orders, and seagulls squawking from the patio railing, there would definitely be no eavesdropping. When Susan grabbed her cell phone and disappeared inside the eatery, I had the sudden urge to find the restroom.

Dropping my menu beside my rolled silverware, I trailed my hand along Ethan's back and followed Susan. Experience had told me to play as dumb as I needed to in order to garner information. Looking for a restroom worked as well as any other excuse.

Susan ducked into a small hallway under a sign

reading 'Women', then through a door. I counted to three, then followed. Hallelujah, she was in one of the two stalls. I locked myself in the other one.

"I told you I didn't think that was the proper way to handle it." Susan sighed over the rustle of paper. "There are better ways when you're on an island. That type of behavior upsets David."

Better ways to do what? Kill someone? I clapped a hand over my mouth to stifle a gasp. Did she mean by shark? Drowning? Horror! Susan was right. An island surrounded by water hosted a million ways to murder someone. Who was she talking to?

I chewed the French tip of my pinkie nail. I would have answered, if anyone asked, that Susan's partner in crime was David. Was he really just an acquaintance? A boyfriend? What about Manano? So many questions.

If Susan was my murderer, and it was way too early in the game to tell, what was her motive? I leaned against the stall wall, then realized I hadn't made any 'bathroom' noises. I flushed the toilet.

When her door opened, I held my breath and shrank back, almost tempted to put my feet on the toilet seat.

"I'll talk to you later. Meet me tonight in the usual place."

Once I knew for sure she had left, I ventured from my hiding place. If she wasn't talking about offing someone, then what was she talking about? Her conversation sounded highly suspect, given the recent circumstances. Maybe I needed to check what type of vehicle she rode in to Lahaina.

Her giggle reached me before I stepped on the patio. She batted eyelashes at Ethan, one hand on her white cotton short-covered hip. April glared at her. Joe stared impassively. Ethan looked like a deer caught in headlights.

I slipped past her and into my seat where I leaned on Ethan's shoulder. "Hello, Susan."

"Summer." Her smile faded, and her eyes narrowed. She glanced over her shoulder at the building, most likely trying to determine whether I was the other person in the ladies room. I lifted my chin. So what. She didn't own the toilet facilities.

"What brings you to Lahaina?" I rested my chin on Ethan's shoulder. His arm snaked around my waist.

"Vacation." With a flick of her hair, she stormed back to her table, murmured something to David, who glowered, then the two left without ordering food.

I shrugged. No skin off my teeth. I picked my menu back up and decided on a tropical salad and glass of iced tea.

"Learn anything on your snooping expedition?" Joe asked.

"Maybe." I grinned at each of them. "Seems Susan is a bit upset about how something was handled and that the same something could have been handled better considering they are on an island."

"That's it?" He reached for his glass of water.

"For now." With today's sleuthing finished, I could enjoy the rest of our time in Lahaina, even if I did have my bulldog of a cousin helping Ethan guard me. "I took it to mean there were better ways of poisoning someone. Like a water-related death, possibly."

"We don't even know if Susan is behind

Jamison's death. Also, she isn't the only guest at the bed and breakfast. We also don't—"

I held up a hand to stop him. "There's a lot we don't know, but it's a start." He sure could bust my bubble faster than anyone. But I had proved my nay-saying cousin wrong three times before, and would do it again. I just needed to bide my time and keep my eyes and ears open. "After we eat, I'd like to visit that gallery across the street."

By that evening, I was sunburned and happy, languishing on my patio, feet up and a pineapple drink in my hand with the handsomest man in Hawaii while the scent of salt water and seaweed teased my nostrils. This was the life!

The art gallery had filled my mind with beauty that almost rivaled the ocean view I gazed on now. Ethan had even been a sweetheart and handed over a few hundred dollars on a tropical painting by a local artist. I couldn't wait to see it displayed in our bedroom back home. I was going to redecorate the room to be a romantic tropical sanctuary.

I took a sip of my drink and puckered at its tartness. "Isn't God's creation glorious?"

A mauve and purple sky stretched across an indigo ocean. Outlines of palm trees stood in stark contrast to the sky. I couldn't believe this was our third night on the island.

Ethan dozed beside me. I transferred my attention back to the water where a couple strolled along the beach. As hissed whispers drifted my way, it occurred to me that they stormed along the water's edge rather than strolled. I narrowed my eyes. It looked to me as if the couple were the other newlyweds, Bruce and Maryann Franklin. I hadn't seen much of them, but if body language was any indication, it appeared as if the honeymoon rode on stormy waves.

When Bruce grabbed Maryann by the arm, Ethan stirred. "I'm watching. Don't let on. I want to see if I need to butt in."

"You shouldn't have done that!" Maryann's voice rose on the breeze. "The man didn't do anything wrong."

"Stay out of what doesn't concern you." Bruce faced the ocean.

"Look at me when I'm talking to you." She put a hand on his arm.

He shrugged free and whirled around, putting his hands on Maryann's shoulders. "If you don't stay out of what doesn't concern you, I can't be responsible for the consequences."

Ethan shifted.

My gentle giant didn't rile easily, but when he did, watch out world. I prayed Bruce wouldn't do anything that signified harm to Maryann. Ethan wasn't the type to sit back while a man mistreated a woman. Me, on the other hand, sipped harder through my straw and kept my gaze glued to the drama unfolding. Of course, if Bruce showed too much aggression toward Maryann, I would be right there on the beach next to Ethan.

Maryann raised her hand to strike.

Bruce took her two in his.

"I'm getting uncomfortable." Ethan stretched then took my hand. "I think it's time for a stroll of our own."

I set my drink on the small glass-topped table and

slipped my feet into flip-flops. "Good idea. If they know there's an audience, they won't fight."

"That's the plan." He tucked my arm close to his side and led me off a ways then doubled back.

My sneaky fella. Didn't want them to know we were watching.

They pulled apart as we neared.

"Hey, you two." Ethan held out his hand to Bruce. "How's the honeymoon?"

"Wonderful." Bruce's grin looked more like a grimace as he returned Ethan's shake.

Maryann crossed her arms and ignored us to the point of walking off and moving into the water.

I shrugged. When I was upset, I didn't want anyone bothering me either, but while the guys talked about whatever guys talked about, I watched her. She hadn't even kicked off her shoes. I frowned. Something was definitely not right.

"Maryann." I kicked off my flip-slops, the sand cool on the soles of my feet, and hoisted my sundress above my knees. The wind picked up, whipping my hair into my eyes. "Plan on swimming in the dark?"

"Go away, Mrs. Banning."

"You can call me Summer. We're around the same age."

"I said go away." Soon she had progressed to the point where the water reached her armpits.

"Seriously, Maryann, this isn't wise." I'd heard of sharks, barracudas, and … piranhas didn't live in these waters, did they? I tried peering through the dark water. Maybe I should have done more research.

Where did she go? I dropped my dress and splashed. "Maryann!" I couldn't see her anywhere. "Ethan! Bruce!"

Fierce splashing sounded behind me.

"I was talking to her one minute, the next, she was gone." Tears clogged my throat. She couldn't drown that fast, could she?

"Wait. I see her." Ethan dove under the water.

"Where?" Bruce shoved water aside. "Maryann! Don't do this to me."

"Do what?" I grabbed his arm.

He yanked free. "Kill herself."

8

Ethan dragged a sputtering Maryann to the surface. She fought to free herself, raining punches on his head and shoulders that didn't appear to have much significance. With a firm jaw, he sloshed toward shore. I moved deeper to help him but Bruce shoved past and pulled her from Ethan's arms.

"What were you thinking?" He cradled her close. "Are you that upset over something that can't be undone?" He splashed his way to shore and set her on her feet.

Ethan took my hand in his and led me to dry ground. We watched as Bruce covered Maryann's face with kisses. Already the wind was drying my skirt into salty stiffness. Sand clung to my feet.

"I'll take care of it. No one will know. I'll hide the evidence," Bruce promised.

I glanced up at Ethan. My list of suspects grew longer with each day. Susan and David spoke about 'other ways' and the Franklins about hiding evidence. In what kind of place had Ethan and I chosen to spend our honeymoon? I almost believed Joe was right in saying that trouble followed me like a fat boy after an ice cream cone.

Lights soon flickered on in the cottages and guests converged on the beach. Mrs. Wahine strolled among them, probably trying to reassure everyone that things would be okay. Mr. Wahine, accompanied by his son, Leroy, bustled their way to us.

"What happened?" Mr. Wahine stood beside Ethan.

"It seems as if she tried to drown herself," Ethan said. "At least, according to her husband's reaction."

"One more thing to put a disparaging light on the B & B." Leroy crossed his arms. "First Mr. Jamison, and now this."

I frowned. "That's a horrible way of looking at it. One person is dead and another almost." How selfish could one young man be?

"Stay out of things that don't concern you." He glared. "This is my future we're talking about."

"That's enough, young man." Ethan shook his head, reverting to his high school football coach tone-of-voice. Only a fool would argue with him when he was in that mode.

"Settle down, son." Mr. Wahine moved to the Franklins, most likely to offer them a free night of their stay, too. If things kept happening as they were, the Wahine's would make very little money this week.

Money was a big motivator for murder.

Did evil lurk behind the round, friendly faces of our hosts? But, if they killed off their guests or guests left because of unpleasant circumstances that would defeat the purpose of acquiring funds. I felt like I was in the wash cycle of a washing machine, tossing and turning with no way of straightening out the clues.

Joe and April joined us, and I filled them in on

the night's happenings.

"Do you think this is all related to Jamison?" I asked.

"How could it be?" Joe shook his head. "A murder and a suicide attempt with witnesses. Not the same at all."

"Maybe Maryann knows something about the murder and the guilt made her want to drown herself." Take that, bossy cousin.

He smirked. "A bit dramatic, don't you think?"

I loved my cousin dearly, but sometimes I wondered how he became a cop. How could you investigate a crime when you walked around with your eyes closed? It was as plain as day, these incidents were related. What were the odds of a murder and a suicide in paradise?

"Shouldn't someone call the police?" Mrs. Aldrich pulled a terry robe closer around her rotund middle. "Suicide is against the law, isn't it? I think I read that somewhere."

Bruce cursed. "She just went for a swim. There's no need for the police." With his arm around his wife, he led her, tottering and sobbing, back to the cottage.

"Looks like Summer went swimming, too." Susan simpered. "Maybe night swims are all the rage."

I bit back a retort that would give me reason to repent later, and instead, smiled. "The water is wonderful. You should try it." I lifted my chin and strode, as nonchalantly as a stiffening dress would allow, to my room.

Ethan and the rest of the family followed. So much for a romantic evening. Everyone would want to hash over the most recent events. At this rate, Ethan and I wouldn't have any newlywed privacy until we returned home. I slammed through the door and marched to the bathroom.

What was wrong with me? I slipped out of my sundress and turned on the shower. Help solving a mystery was always welcome. What I resented was the timing.

Having managed to keep myself chaste until the ripe old age of thirty, it didn't take more than the first night to show me how much I enjoyed what transpired between a man and a woman. I didn't like having others interfere with spontaneity.

I sighed and stepped under the shower head, allowing the warm water to wash away the sea salt and my self-pity. The family could have one hour, then I would kick them out.

By the time I entered the living area in my silky pajamas and robe, the others were crowded around the table with a pad of paper and a pen.

Joe glanced up. "You're good at making lists. Here's what we have so far."

He was actually asking for my input? "Who do you have?"

"Nobody, actually. One of us always comes up with a reason to discount them. We're doing more arguing than work."

"You're a cop." I settled in an empty chair. "Take charge."

"I'm on vacation."

Good grief. I glanced at Ethan, who shrugged. I blew him a kiss and focused on the task at hand.

"Put down Susan Wood and David Hatcher. Also, Bruce and Maryann Franklin. The Wahine's—"

"That sweet old couple?" Aunt Eunice waved away the thought. "Never."

Joe wrote them down.

"Don't forget their kids." I chewed my pinky nail. "The maid, and Camilla Wahine. She found the body." What about the Aldrich's? I decided to ask some questions. "So far, everyone outside of this room is a suspect."

"The Wahine's buy their nuts from a candy shop in Lahaina," Joe said as he wrote. "Manano checked them out and thinks the nuts were clean when the Wahine's got them."

"Put him down, too." I pointed at the paper.

"He's a police officer." Joe glowered.

"A dirty one, I'd bet my next pineapple."

"I agree with Summer," Ethan said, standing. "There's something that doesn't sit right about him. Anyone want something to drink?"

All hands went up.

"Six glasses of water all around."

Bless my husband. He knew if he handed out tasty drinks, they'd all stay forever.

"The folks I still want to investigate are the gardener and the Aldrichs."

"I don't like it. Not one bit," Aunt Eunice said. "But you know me, I mind my own business. We're just here for moral support."

I almost laughed out loud. She had been involved in all three of previous jaunts into crime solving.

"I think you girls should let the men handle this. It's too dangerous. Don't forget, I got stabbed last time." Uncle Roy lifted his tropical print shirt and showed us the scar. A raw pucker that marred his pasty-white skin.

"That was because of an elephant, not a murderer." I accepted the glass Ethan handed me and smiled, lifting my face for a kiss.

He obliged and continued around the table.

"Which of these people fit the sweats?" April took her glass and set it on the table. "Wouldn't that rule out some of these people?"

"That is an excellent point." Aunt Eunice raised her hand for a high five.

I shook my head. She forgot she was in her sixties until she tried to keep up with me. I loved her dearly and waited my turn to high-five.

"Tomorrow, we're going to the volcano. Are we going to watch the sunset or rise? I heard the Aldrichs say at supper that they were going up there and making a day of it." Aunt Eunice stood. "I've made a point of befriending the woman. She's a kind soul, but I'll try to get her to talk, if you think she killed someone."

"She's a suspect, Eunice," Joe said. "Nothing more."

"Well, if she tries something, I'll throw her into the fiery pit."

"It's a dormant volcano." Joe's face reddened. "And you can't make threats."

"I can say what I darn well please." She planted her fists on her hips. "If anyone tries any funny business, I'll give them what-for!"

Okay. I stood and started gathering glasses. "Sounds like we've got a busy day ahead of us. Time to get to sleep. I seriously doubt we'll make it for sunrise."

"I'm too riled up to sleep, thanks to your cousin." Aunt Eunice glared. "He does go on with his nonsense like a silly fool."

"Well, try anyway." I gave her a pointed look.

Could she not take a hint?

"Oh." She paled and grabbed Uncle Roy's hand. "They are…you know…um…"

"On their honeymoon." He grinned. "I get it. Let's go, old woman." He kissed her cheek and ushered her out, followed by Joe and April.

Ethan closed the door behind them and turned with a grin. "Your family is as much fun as a circus."

"A regular riot." I set the glasses in the sink, grateful that we had splurged on a cabin with all the amenities in case we didn't want to join the others for meals. I suppose it gave honeymooners the chance to practice real married life.

Although, I doubted many of them planned on solving a murder while enjoying that so-called life.

9

I was glad we'd opted for watching the sun set instead of rise. Something about the legend of the demigod Maui lassoing the sun to make the day last longer, resonated with me far more than forcing myself to rise early. The beauty of the land invited a person to linger and enjoy God's creation, not rush helter-skelter through the day like life on the mainland.

"Ready?" Ethan stowed a small ice chest in the back of the van and closed the rear door. He eyed my bare legs. "I've heard it's pretty chilly up there. Maybe you should wear long pants."

"I didn't bring any. This is Hawaii. It's tropical."

"Do you have a sweater?"

Wasn't he listening? Aunt Eunice, a windbreaker draped over her arm, bustled down the walk accompanied by April, who wore yoga pants with a sweater tied around her waist.

"It gets cold up there," Aunt Eunice said. "Flip-flops and shorts will not do according to the Wahines."

I sighed. "I've got gym shoes inside. Be right back."

After setting my camera on the van seat, I hurried inside the cottage and changed into a flower print maxi sundress over a white tee shirt. At least the dress would cover my legs. Then, I slipped on pink and white gym shoes which looked ridiculous with the predominantly red dress.

When I rejoined the others, Aunt Eunice shoved some pea green soup-colored sweater at me, that once I put it on, would swallow me whole. So much for fashion.

"Let's go." Joe clapped his hands together then rubbed them. "Time to get this show on the road. It'll take about two hours to get there from here. Hope y'all don't get car sick."

"Car sick?" Of course I did. Joe knew that, too, as evidenced by the grin he gave as he climbed into the front seat. Again. A person would think he was the one who married Ethan. I didn't get nearly as sick if I rode in the front.

I dug into my purse, pulled out my nausea pills, and grinned. Since we planned on possibly taking a boat somewhere to snorkel rather than right off shore every time, I had come prepared. I waved the packet in his face, then settled back in my seat and popped one in my mouth.

"Grow up, Summer." Joe faced forward.

"Where's the fun in that?" I focused on the glorious scene outside.

We passed fields of pineapple and pastures of fat cattle. We stopped and waited while a school bus dropped off children. I smiled at the sight of little girls in sundresses and flip-flops. If not for the murder, life on Maui would seem idyllic.

The whole concept of living on an island didn't

bother me. You might not be able to drive to the coast in a day in Arkansas, but I still didn't think being surrounded by water would suffocate me. Especially when the water was such a brilliant blue, flowers abounded, life slowed down, and people were friendly.

By the time we were halfway up the volcano, I thanked God profusely for the nausea medicine. The road was so curvy it often turned back on itself. I had heard the road to Hana was treacherous. If it was worse than this, I'd be white-knuckled the entire trip.

I wrapped my arms around the headrest and massaged Ethan's shoulders. There didn't seem to be enough physical affection between us for a honeymoon. I cast a sideways glance at the others. No one needed to tell me why there was a lack.

"Parking lot is full." Ethan slowed.

"There." Joe pointed. "By the gift shop."

The moment I climbed from the van, the wind whipped my hair around my face and my skirt around my legs with a biting force. The cold cut to the bone, even after I wrestled myself into Aunt Eunice's giant sweater. For once, I was glad to be wrong about my previous choice of attire.

Ethan grabbed my hand. "Do you want to observe the crater from the store window?"

"No. I want to take pictures." I headed for the railing. "Oh, look. We're in heaven."

The clouds below us looked thick enough to walk on. All they lacked was a cherub with wings and a harp. In the distance, a rainbow cut through the clouds completing the fantasy picture. Although I knew the camera wouldn't do the sight justice, I snapped a few pictures and chose to do my best to ignore the wind.

"I'm up. We'll meet at O one hundred hours to compare notes." Aunt Eunice clapped me on the shoulder and pushed her way into the store where the Aldrich's milled with a few other tourists.

"I'd best make sure she doesn't cause a ruckus." Uncle Roy followed his eager wife.

Joe shook his head and grabbed April's hand. "Let's take a look at the crater."

Finally alone. Just as I preferred. I turned and beamed at Ethan. "I want to see the crater, too. Let's walk off a ways."

His arm around my shoulders felt warm and comforting, steadying me. Why wasn't there a brochure in our room warning us of the temperature and weather up here? I pressed closer and let him lead me to a spot relatively free of tourists.

I leaned my elbows on the rail. It did indeed look like the moon. Black dirt mingled with hues of rust, smaller craters within the large one, plants I'd never seen before with spiky silver leaves. I laid eyes on another planet. If not for people starting to crowd close, I could almost believe I had entered another world. What a contrast from the lushness below.

When Joe and April joined us, I stepped away, not willing to give up that strange sense of otherworldliness. I snapped picture after picture, hoping they would look as fantastic when I printed them.

People crowded closer, smashing me against the iron rail. I shoved back. Someone banged into me. My hip slammed against the rail. Pain shot through me. I tried peering over the crowd for Ethan.

I was lifted off my feet.

I tried to turn around. Someone had me tight against the railing, slowly shoving me over. The crater floor looked miles away. My heart stopped.

No way could someone survive the fall. With so many people crowded around, it would look like an accident.

Adrenaline prickled my skin. My breath came in gasps. I kicked backwards and screamed.

The pressure released. I fell in a lump on the ground. The crowd moved back as Ethan forced his way through.

"Summer!" He knelt and pulled me close. "Are you hurt?"

"Someone tried to push me over."

"Are you sure? It's gotten very crowded, maybe it was an accident." He pulled me to my feet.

"Like the spear?" I gripped his arms. "Was that an accident? Ethan, I'll have bruises I can show you later to prove someone tried to push me."

His face paled. "Come on. Let's get you in the store."

"I want to sit down. Is there somewhere to sit?" My head swam and despite the temperature, perspiration broke out on my upper lip. No matter how many times somebody tried, I could not get used to someone trying to kill me.

Ethan lowered me to a nearby bench and took a knee. "I'm sorry." He smoothed the hair away from my face. "I shouldn't have let us get separated. We're going home."

"No, the others are enjoying the view."

He took my face in his hands. "I mean home. Mountain Springs, Arkansas."

"No." I bolted to my feet. Tears stung my eyes.

"We're on our honeymoon."

"I can't spend it in fear for your safety." He wiped away the escaping tears with his thumbs.

I locked gazes with him. I could drown in his blue eyes. What should I do? Agree to go home or stay and pray God kept me safe? I'd been locked in a trunk before, chased at gunpoint through a carnival funhouse, and dropped into a dry well. A Hawaiian island offered a whole new sphere of dangerous ways for a person to try to murder me.

But did I want to go home yet? I glanced down the summit. The clouds separated, offering a glimpse of Maui in all her glory. No, I wasn't ready to go home. I'd have to be more diligent and do my best not to further anger whoever thought I was mixed up in all this … whatever *it* was.

"No, I want to stay."

Ethan expelled a rough breath. "I wish you would reconsider."

I cupped his cheek. "When we go back, our lives are crazy again. You've got school and coaching, I've got the store to run. Let me live in fantasy land a little longer. I'll stay glued to your side, which isn't hard now that we're married." My attempt at a flirty smile failed, instead wavering and calling attention to my false attitude of serenity. Inside, my nerves twanged like an out of tune guitar.

"That was a waste of time." Aunt Eunice plopped next to me. "That woman is a real good liar. Nobody can be that chipper all the time." Her eyes narrowed. "What's the matter with you?"

"Somebody tried to push her over the railing into the crater." Planting his hands on his thighs, Ethan pushed to his feet.

"What?" Joe stomped up. "Are you sure?"

"Of course I'm sure." Could he not, just once, believe me outright without my having to prove myself?

"Where were you?" Uncle Roy put his arm around me. "Why weren't you looking out for our girl?"

Ethan's jaw clenched

"I wandered off to take pictures." I slipped free and stood by Ethan. "While I appreciate your concern, Uncle Roy, I'm Ethan's girl now."

His eyes reddened. "You'll always be my girl. A ring on your finger won't change that."

A mountain set up residence in my throat. "I love you, Uncle Roy. You, too, Aunt Eunice, but Ethan is perfectly capable of watching out for me."

"Maybe I'm not." He glanced down. "If I hadn't been close enough to hear you scream, you could have gone over before anyone knew you were even in danger." He ran his fingers through his windswept hair. "I think we should go back, but Summer says no."

"I don't think I would want to let the killer win, either," April said. "It's bad enough you have all of us here on your honeymoon. I say you go about things as if nothing happened. Don't get involved in gathering information or anything. Just have fun and keep one eye peeled behind you."

"Or," Aunt Eunice added. "We solve this darn thing and enjoy the rest of the trip."

I kind of liked that idea. "What did you find about Mrs. Aldrich?"

"Other than that she is infernally happy?" Aunt Eunice crossed her arms. "Nothing. Boy howdy, it's chilly out here."

"Yes, but so beautiful." I slipped my hand into Ethan's. "I'd like one more look before we go, okay?"

He nodded and led me to the crater. He positioned me in front of him and leaned against my back, one arm on each side, providing a protective barrier.

I looked down. Way down, and gave thanks to God that I wasn't a part of that awesome landscape. I leaned into Ethan's strong chest.

"I want to stay and find out who is trying to kill me." I turned and stared into his face. "If I don't, I'll always wonder. Always be looking over my shoulder."

He nodded and blinked rapidly before pulling me tight to his chest. "You scare me to death."

10

"Here." April slipped my tazer into my hand right before I entered my cottage. "I brought it as soon as we knew what was going on out here. Thought you might need it."

"Thanks." I hugged her. "You're the best." I slipped the small box-shaped object onto the entry table by the door the moment I followed Ethan into the room.

He sat in the armchair, head in his hands.

My heart melted at the sight of him so dejected, so worried. Maybe we should go home. It was selfish of me to put him through this. A knock sounded at the door, stopping me from uttering words I really didn't want to say.

I turned. Officer Manano, accompanied by his sidekick, Williams, stood on the sidewalk. "Officers, how may I help you?"

"This is not a pleasure call, Mrs. Banning." Officer Manano pushed past me. "So, I will get straight to the point. Did you visit Haleakala Crater today?"

"Yes." Had someone told him about my close

escape from death? My gaze fell on the tazer. I stepped in front of the table and slid the object behind the lamp. It wouldn't do for Officer Five-O to confiscate my only weapon.

"Did you speak to Mrs. Aldrich?" He nodded to Williams, who pulled a notepad and pen from his pocket.

"No, I did not. Why would you ask me that?"

"What's this about?" Ethan stood next to me.

"Mrs. Aldrich is dead. Someone thought she needed to dry her hair while taking a bath."

"What?" Was this building too old to have a breaker that would trip if an electrical appliance fell in the water? I glanced toward the bathroom. "Isn't there a code or something that prevents buildings from being archaic enough to allow someone to be electrocuted?"

"Apparently not," he answered.

"Someone needs to check into that." Seriously. Someone else could be killed.

He peered at me from under thick brows. "I'll get right on it."

My legs refused to hold me. I collapsed onto the sofa. "She was so happy earlier."

"I thought you didn't speak with her." Manano leaped on my words like a bird on a June bug.

"I didn't, my —" I ducked my head, not wanting to give up my aunt to this man I didn't trust.

"Your   what?"
"Aunt." I sighed. "Aunt Eunice said Mrs. Aldrich was happier than anyone had a right to be." Why did I feel like a stool pigeon? Anyone in their right mind would know Aunt Eunice couldn't kill anyone. Well, maybe a deer or a rabbit, but nothing human. Poor Mr.

Aldrich. He must be devastated. He and his wife had seemed so in love with each other.

Williams's pen scratched the surface of the paper. When I craned to see what he wrote, he turned away.

"Any reason your aunt might want to stop Mrs. Aldrich from being so happy?"

"That's pure ridiculousness."

Manano gave me a cold stare. "I sincerely hope you aren't planning on leaving Maui any time soon, Mrs. Banning."

Well, there went Ethan's opportunity to spirit me away.

"Not before the thirteenth," Ethan said. "By then, we'll all know for sure who the killer is." The frigid tone of his voice gave me goose bumps.

The two men stared unblinking until Manano turned away. "Stay out of police business. There's more going on than you know."

From the determined look on Ethan's face, I knew he was set on finding out just what that was. The thought scared me a bit. He had helped me a lot in the last two mysteries I solved, but with this one, he might be even more fixated than me.

After the police left, Ethan turned to me. "Let's go."

"Where?"

He tugged me to my feet. "I need to talk to Joe. We need to come up with a plan to solve this thing before you're either killed or thrown in jail."

Neither option appealed to me, so I slipped my feet back into the flip-flops that had slipped off when I plopped to the sofa, and followed my husband outside.

No sun peeked through the trees as it said

farewell to the day. Instead, the moon hovered above an inky ocean. Water lapped the shoreline with the relaxing sounds of waves against sand. A paradise soured by two deaths.

"We weren't home for long, Ethan." I quick-stepped to keep up with him. "Someone needed easy access to Mrs. Aldrich. I think we need to look closer at her husband."

He peered at me. "You don't think he's too obvious?"

"Maybe he wants the police to think just that."

"What's his motive?"

I shrugged. "That's the million dollar question." I slipped my hand in his, loving the feel of his callouses.

No lights shined from my family's cottages.

"Let's go down to the beach." I squeezed Ethan's hand. "We have a suspect list. The two of us can maybe come up with some motives."

"Maybe. But it'll be tough without asking some questions." He turned toward the main building. "What do you think about trying to get into Mr. Jamison's room?"

"You mean illegal entry?" I grinned. "I'm all for it!"

"Shhh." He laughed and pulled me behind a bush. "We need a plan."

"We can be drunk newlyweds looking for our room. Maybe no one will be around other than the maid, and she might not know exactly where we're staying. I haven't run into her much." Adrenaline coursed through me. I didn't think, God forgive me, I could ever get tired of spying on people or sneaking into places I wasn't supposed to be.

Most likely, I'd have to answer to God someday but I was certain He would understand. After all, He gave me my insatiable curiosity.

"Do you know how to act drunk?" Ethan's eyes twinkled in the moonlight.

"I've seen actors do it. How hard can it be?"

"Let's just be so engrossed in each other that we are oblivious to anyone around us."

"That will work too." I slipped my arm through his and snuggled close. "Lead on, handsome husband of mine."

"We need a glimpse of the guest book to see which room is his," Ethan said. "Pray it's left where we can find it."

The foyer of the Bed and Breakfast was empty. The dining room was set for breakfast. The living room was dark but for a single lamp burning. I remembered Mrs. Wahine saying guests were welcome to sit and read at any hour of the day or night. Closed on the welcome desk was a burgundy leather book.

"That's it." These people were either very trusting or very stupid. I flipped open the cover to April 3 and ran my finger down the page. "Here it is. He was in cottage number two."

"Back of the property. Convenient for a killer." Ethan pulled me along with him and out the double French doors leading to the cottages farther away from the ocean.

"Who has access to the nuts?"

His steps slowed. "Nuts?"

"The gift box that's given to every guest. Wasn't he poisoned by them?" We continued our walk. "Do we know what kind of poison?"

"Maybe Joe can find out. It would have to be something undetectable by the guest."

I know if I wanted to poison someone, I would use plain old easy-to-get rat poison. Or arsenic, maybe. Anything I could dilute in water and inject into something would be my weapon of choice. If I were a murderer, that is.

We stopped in front of cottage number two. Yellow crime scene tape, having come loose from a nearby bush, waved an eerie welcome in the night breeze. Not a good advertisement for the Wahine B & B.

I figured the front door would be locked, but used the hem of my dress to turn the handle anyway. Yep. Locked. Ethan motioned toward the side of the building.

Staying in the shadows, we made our way to the back where approximately two feet above my head was the bathroom window. Open and beckoning us to enter.

"Give me a boost." I put my hands on Ethan's shoulders. "Once I get inside, I'll unlock the door for you."

"No, open a bedroom window. I don't want to be seen going in the front door." He hefted me up and almost tossed me through and onto my head. My flip-flops fell outside somewhere.

It wasn't until I stood up, that I realized Mr. Jamison had died in the bathroom. The very room where I now stood barefoot. Eeew. I rose on the balls of my feet. Had they laid his body here after pulling him from the tub?

The tub.

I forgot my squeamishness and stared through the

gloom into the white porcelain coffin shaped tub.

Both Mr. Jamison and Mrs. Aldrich had died in their bathtubs.

11

I would *not* take a bath while on Maui.

"Summer, let me in." Ethan's loud whisper drifted through the open window.

I padded out of the bathroom and into the bedroom where I shoved up the window. "Sorry. I was transfixed by the tub. Are you aware both deaths occurred while taking a bath? I'm so glad I'm a shower person, because no one is going to convince me to take a bath on this island."

"I love you, you silly goose. I never know what you're going to say." He pulled me back into the bathroom. "Now, what?"

"What do you mean?"

"What do we do next? You're the expert."

Usually I stumbled across evidence by accident. I considered it a strange gift from God. I chewed my pinkie nail. "Look for anything out of the ordinary." I turned in a slow circle and kept my eyes open.

The bed lay unmade. A rumpled towel lay on the bathroom floor. A popular brand of men's shower gel and deodorant sat on the lip of the tub. Discarded clothes were on the floor by the sink.

A box of chocolate-covered macadamia nuts sat

on the bedroom dresser. I dashed into the bathroom and glanced at the empty counter. Next to the tub, someone had pulled up a vanity stool. To set a different gift box of nuts on, perhaps? And the outlet sported a lovely red button to prevent electrocution when dropped in the water. I started to think Office Manano had lied to us about Mrs. Aldrich's death. Wasn't it building code to have outlets updated?

Manano definitely fed us false information to try and determine how much we really knew about these two deaths.

"Ethan?"

"Yeah." His voice came from the closet.

"Did we get more than one box of nuts?"

He appeared in the doorway. "What?"

I grabbed his hand and pulled him toward the dresser. "I'm no genius, but I'm pretty sure the police would have taken the poisoned nuts. Why does Mr. Jamison have more than one complimentary box?"

"Maybe he bought one."

"Maybe, but I don't think so." I propped on the edge of the bed. The box was stamped with the Wahine Bed and Breakfast logo. The hotel didn't have a gift shop, so purchasing the box didn't sound feasible to me. "The police obviously took the box that contained the nuts that killed him." It seemed strange to me that they would leave this one here, untested, but I'd seen stranger things. "We need to talk to the maid."

"In a minute." Ethan pulled a folded sheet of paper from the closet. "I found this in an inner pocket of a suit. It's an email about building a resort in Kihei, and it isn't a very nice one."

"Here? Where the B & B is?"

"Maybe." Ethan sat beside me. "That could give us a possible motive."

I skimmed the printed message. "It reads more like a hate letter. Mr. Jamison seems to have stiffed someone in regards to the proposed resort. We need to find out who."

"Then we have our killer." Ethan took the paper from me.

"That's what I'm hoping." I still had no idea why someone wanted to kill me, though. It couldn't be because I was in the wrong place at the wrong time. That made absolutely no sense.

"I'm going to show this to Joe." He slipped the letter into the back pocket of his jeans.

I grinned. "I've corrupted you. You're tampering with possible evidence."

"Only to keep my girl safe." He pulled me to my feet and into his arms. "Let's get some sleep. We can try the maid in the morning."

###

I rolled over and pounded my pillow for the umpteenth time. The thought that the attempts on me weren't because of Jamison's murder, or even Mrs. Aldrich's, wouldn't leave me.

My first attempt at crime solving had been an accident. Diamonds buried under my prize rosebush. The second, a family affair because of the first. The third mystery turned out to be a love triangle slash computer scam and had nothing to do with the previous two. How did the two current deaths relate to me? Did they? Were they tied in to my prior crime solving, or complete coincidence?

I stopped tossing and stared at Ethan. I lightly traced his lips with my finger and then ran my hand over the stubble on his cheek. Although having him along while I tried solving a mystery and keeping myself alive, I worried. What if I caused him to be hurt? Or worse? I would jump off the volcano if that happened. A fiery lava death would be too easy for me.

"That tickles." Ethan smiled and opened his eyes. "Can't sleep?"

I shook my head.

"Wanna talk about it?" He leaned on his elbow, his dark gaze searching my face.

"Our honeymoon's been ruined!" A sob threatened to choke off my words. "That's a selfish thought, isn't it?" I wiped my eyes on the sheet, leaving a trace of mascara behind. "But I can't help it. Every time we leave this room, someone tries to kill me. What if they hurt you in the process?"

"We could just stay in the cottage." He winked. "We're safe here."

"I'm being serious."

"I'm sorry." He pulled me close for a kiss. "The honeymoon isn't ruined, just more exciting. We'll still see the sights we wanted, but in a group. And, we'll solve this thing before we go home."

"How can you be so certain?" I sniffed.

"I just am." He pulled me close. "I've got something that will help you sleep."

Yes, I knew he did. I closed my eyes and pressed closer.

###

Someone pounded on the door.

I jerked to a sitting position and squinted against the sun squeezing through the slats in the blinds. One glance at the clock told me I'd slept in, as had Ethan.

Something I rarely did. I stretched, remembering our time of lovemaking, then shook Ethan awake. "Someone's at the door."

He groaned. "If that's your family, call the police, because I'm going to kill them." In one fluid motion, he wrapped the sheet around him and climbed from bed. "I ought to go out there stark naked and show them what they interrupt when they knock on the door of honeymooners."

My face flamed. "We were sleeping."

"We could have been doing something else."

I burrowed deeper in the pillows. I did love my grouchy morning bear, and agreed with him that if it was my family pounding on the door, they needed to learn boundaries. Wait. What if it wasn't them?

"Ethan? What if it isn't Aunt Eunice or Uncle Roy? What if it's the killer?"

He glanced over his shoulder at me. "Hide in the bathroom." He wrapped his fist around the lamp and yanked it from the wall. "If you hear a ruckus, call the police."

Taking the blankets with me, I scuttled to the bathroom and slammed the door. I hated hiding like a frightened child. The tiny room had nothing I could use as a weapon. Mine or Ethan's razor would be of little help. I supposed I could brandish the toilet brush and throw an attacker off guard.

"Summer, it's your family." Ethan's disgruntled voice came through the door. "Get dressed."

Heavens! Their timing wasn't the best, but still wonderful considering. Although, I suppose most killers wouldn't bother to knock.

When I walked into the small living room, all heads turned in my direction. Ethan raised his eyebrows and shrugged as if to tell me there wasn't much he could do to keep everyone out. Joe's face resembled a tomato.

"What did I do now?" I headed for the tiny kitchen for a glass of water.

"You and Ethan were seen going into Jamison's cottage." Joe crossed his arms. "You put my friend up to this, didn't you?"

"Wait a minute—" Ethan stood.

Joe held up a hand. "It's okay, buddy. I know my cousin, and she can be quite enticing when she wants to be."

I cocked my head and decided not to respond to his outrageous accusations. Instead, I guzzled my drink like I didn't have a care in the world and silently rejoiced at April's warning look toward Joe.

"Who saw us?" Ethan frowned.

"I did."

"Well, if it was you, what's the big deal?" Ethan plopped back to the sofa.

"The deal, sweetheart..." I took my time moseying my way over to the group. "Is that my cousin likes to be dramatic. He spends his time being nosey and is stung by the fact that we actually gained entrance. Obviously he tried and didn't. Isn't that right, Joe?"

His face darkened to the point I thought he might have a stroke.

"He's too big to fit through the window and wouldn't think about asking April to help." I patted his shoulder on my way to balance on the arm of the sofa next to Ethan. "Well?"

"You're right. Partially. I chose not to break and enter when I discovered the front door locked." He pouted. "How do you get away with that type of behavior?"

"Lucky, I guess." I tossed him a grin. "Besides, I now have Ethan's help."

Joe sighed. "Did you find anything?"

"Just the curious fact that apparently Mr. Jamison had two boxes of nuts in his room. One is still sitting on the dresser." I sat my glass on the coffee table with a flourish, enjoying the fact of having 'got one up' on Joe.

Neither one of us really knows when things got so competitive between us and while I know Joe would die for me and me the same for him, life wouldn't be the same if we weren't trying to outdo each other. "And a really mean email from someone called anti-resort-builder who seems to have a grudge against the late Mr. Jamison."

"Y'all did good." Joe rubbed his chin. "Now, we need to decide the next step. You also need to lay low. The last thing you want is to be arrested."

It wouldn't be the first time. "We thought I'd try getting information out of the maid."

"How do you plan on doing that?" Uncle Roy snagged a banana from the fruit basket. "You need to be subtle. You can't just prance up to the girl and say, 'Hey, heard you found the body.'"

"I know that. Besides, Camilla found the body, but maids often know everything that goes on in a place." I twirled my hair "We're suddenly going to be low on towels."

12

"Do you know who the maid is?" Joe asked.

"A young, pretty Hawaiian girl in a muumuu." I grabbed my purse.

"They both are young and pretty and wear muumuus."

"Two maids?" I'd only seen one on the night they found Jamison. "Do you have names?"

"They're sisters. Malia and Micah, I think. Twins. Also, depending on the number of guests, sometimes Camilla helps the maids out." Joe reached for an apple. "Are we going to breakfast? They stop serving in thirty minutes, and I'm starving."

"In a minute. Why would the cops lie about the cause of Mrs. Aldrich's death?" I kept my gaze focused on Joe. No way was I allowing him to give me a mundane answer.

He sighed. "To keep certain pertinent information out of the press." He crossed his arms. "If only the killer knows the truth, the authorities can weed out the thrill seekers and story tellers."

"Did you know from the beginning they were lying?"

"Yes." He looked at me as if I were stupid.

"Nobody dies from a hair dryer in the bath, unless the house is not up to code." He chomped his apple.

Apparently 'everyone' was smarter than me. I grabbed my purse from the counter. "If I'm not back in an hour, call the police."

"Slow down, hot shot." Ethan laid a hand on my arm. "We're going to breakfast. Then, you and I will get up and search for the maid."

I shook my head. "I think April and I should excuse ourselves to go to the restroom. The girl is more likely to talk to women than men."

"I agree." April spoke up. "And since I gave Summer her tazer, then…"

"You did what?" A vein throbbed in Ethan's temple.

April returned his glare. "I brought her tazer. A girl needs to be able to defend herself."

"See, Ethan?" I figured I ought to step in before he really blew up at his sister. "April and I will be just fine. We'll take our cell phones, you'll be waiting in the dining room, and if anything happens, which it won't…" I widened my eyes. "You'll be right there to save us." I flashed a grin.

"If Manano sees you snooping," Joe stood. "And something else happens, you'll only reaffirm his opinion that you are somehow involved in these murders."

"Don't say that about your cousin!" Aunt Eunice slapped him on the arm. "Summer wouldn't hurt a fly and you know it. I've half a mind to help her myself."

Uncle Roy slipped an arm around her ample waist. "Not on our second honeymoon, sweetheart. No risk taking."

"But it's all right for our baby?" She glared.

"We're here, aren't we?" He waggled his eyebrows. "If it makes you feel better, we'll ask some questions at breakfast and supper. Can we eat now?"

Ethan glanced at his watch. "We'd better hurry if we want served."

We hurried outside and to the dining room. April and I exchanged nervous smiles. Although she was always willing to help me in my mystery-solving, I could tell she suffered from a bit of trepidation. I did tend to land us in tight spots.

I reached over and squeezed her hand. "I won't do anything foolhardy. I promise."

"Good." She squeezed back then slipped her arm through Joe's.

It still amazed me how someone so sweet could love my bullheaded cousin, but everyone deserved love, I supposed. Even Joe.

We all took our seats toward the end of the long wooden table. I did my best not to fidget and to wait until I had at least eaten half of my pancakes with mango salsa. I didn't want to appear too eager, nor did I want to miss speaking with the maids while the other guests were occupied.

I motioned to April. "I'm going to the ladies room. Would you like to go with me?"

"What? Are we in Junior High?" Aunt Eunice rolled her eyes. "You can't go to the bathroom alone?"

I gave her a look trying to tell her to be quiet. Had she forgotten so soon that we had a plan? Shaking my head, I led April into the foyer. "Do you think the maids are in the main building or one of the cottages?"

"Let's take a walk. My guess is a cottage. Most

likely they take the opportunity of meal time to clean undisturbed."

With our arms linked, we strolled down the flagstone walk and kept our eyes open for the maid's cart. Wonderful! It sat outside the cottage my family shared.

"We can go in with the excuse of you looking for something." I tugged April with me. *Please, God, let it be the maid who found Mr. Jamison.*

The maid tucked fresh sheet corners under the mattress. She turned with a smile. Thankfully, she was the one I had seen the night of the murder. "I'll be finished in just a moment."

"That's okay. We're just," I grabbed April's camera off the dresser. "Grabbing this."

How could I approach the subject of Mr. Jamison?

She raised her eyebrows. "May I be of service?"

"Well, I, uh." I took a deep breath. "You're Malia, the one who found the man in his bathtub, right?"

"Yes." Her shoulders slumped. "I do not wish to talk about it."

"Please. Just a couple of questions." I motioned for her to sit.

Eyes filling, she nodded and perched on the edge of the bed. "It was the most awful thing I'd ever experienced. He was foaming at the mouth, his lips were blue, eyes bulging..." She shuddered. "The night it happened, Mr. Wahine told us all to act as normal as possible so as to set the guests at ease. It was so hard to smile."

For someone who didn't want to talk, she seemed to have warmed up just fine. I forced my stomach not to rebel.

April clutched her stomach and plopped on the bed beside Malia. "No more description, please."

"Did you notice another box of nuts on the dresser?"

Malia raised a confused face. "Pardon?"

"Other than the box of nuts spilled beside Mr. Jamison's tub, did you see another one?"

"All I saw was the box on the dresser and it was unopened. What are you saying? That there were two complimentary boxes?" She stood and paced. "That's impossible. Those gifts are only accessible by employees of the Wahine's." She withdrew a key from a hidden pocket in her floral uniform. "I must do an inventory right away."

I motioned to April to follow. We'd hit pay dirt! If Malia found an extra box had been used, we would know Mr. Jamison died at the hands of an employee. I couldn't help but grin. This case could be solved within the hour.

"I'm going to text Ethan and let him know what we're doing." April pressed buttons on her cell phone. "Otherwise, he might think he needs to rescue us."

"Good thinking." I increased my pace to match the furious one of Malia. Once she thought there might be a thief on the grounds, she sure had gotten over her despair at finding a dead body mighty quick.

She led us through a back door to the kitchen then into a pantry the size of my bedroom back home. I glanced at the full shelves with envy. The island of Maui could be self-sufficient from the amount of food stored there.

Stopping in front of a towering shelf of little

white and gold boxes, Malia consulted a clipboard then started counting. She chewed her lip, and then counted again.

"Yes," she said. "There is a box missing."

Triumph! Thank God for meticulous inventory.

"This is unacceptable." Malia shook her head. "I need to report this right away."

"We'll come with you."

She stared at me. "Why?"

"Because we alerted you to the fact there might be one missing." I gave her my most innocent look. "This could be invaluable in the authorities solving the murder."

"Okay."

April and I high-fived each other as soon as Malia turned her back to us. I couldn't wait to see the look on Manano's face when we solved the murders.

Once we figured out what had happened to Mr. Jamison, we could move on to Mrs. Aldrich. Although the methods were different, I knew the two deaths were related.

Somehow, I needed to figure out how to find out whether Mrs. Aldrich was actually poisoned, since everyone in the world but me knew she couldn't actually be electrocuted. Maybe I could have April wheedle Joe into finding out. He'd do anything for his 'girl'.

We stopped in front of French doors covered with gauzy fabric. Malia knocked.

"Come in."

Malia pushed open the door and led the way inside a room with a teak wood desk and walls of books. I felt like Belle in Beauty and the Beast.

"Mr. Wahine? I have found a discrepancy in our

inventory I think you should be made aware of." Malia twisted her hands in the folds of her dress. Her face paled.

"Yes?" He frowned.

Was it possible the gentle teddy bear-of-a-man was more like a grizzly bear?

"There is a box of nuts missing."

He shrugged and turned back to the papers on his desk. "Maybe one of my children took it. They enjoy the chocolate."

How could I let him know Ethan and I were in Mr. Jamison's room without being prosecuted for trespassing?

"Mrs. Banning!" As if he just noticed me, his smile returned. "May I help you?"

"No, we just accompanied Malia here. She seemed shaken up. We'll all be leaving now. Thank you." I put my arms around the other girls' shoulders and ushered them from the room. "He doesn't seem concerned about the missing box."

"He is." Malia plopped on a nearby wicker bench. "He is fanatic about knowing where everything is at all times. He tends to blow when a towel is missing, much less expensive nuts." She covered her face. "Oh, he'll think I'm trying to cover up the fact I took them."

I sat next to her. "No, he won't. Not with me and April having gone with you. He has to keep up appearances." He did a really good job, too. Everyone was convinced the portly man was a jolly Hawaiian version of Santa Claus.

"I shouldn't be speaking ill of my employer." Malia stood. "He is only stressed because the Bed and Breakfast is in danger."

"In danger?" I looked at April.

"Someone told me, they want to build a fancy resort here. I must go." Malia scampered away like she was a mouse and us the cats.

"We need to find out what kind of business Mr. Jamison was in."

April nodded. "My guess—development."

The door opened and Mr. Wahine joined us. He startled, almost dropping the ledger in his hand. "Ladies?"

"We were just leaving." I dropped my gaze to the book in his hand. Did it show more red tallies than black?

"No hurry. Other than our private quarters, the Wahine Bed and Breakfast is home to guests. Aloha." He disappeared through a door across the hall.

Was I to assume closed doors were private quarters? I eyed the library, office, whatever he had just come out of. "Did he tell us which were his family's private quarters?"

April smiled. "He neglected that piece of important information."

"Then we return tonight and search this desk."

13

Ethan rubbed his chin as I filled him in on what Malia had told us. I liked the fact he didn't shave everyday while on the island. It gave him a rugged, outdoorsy look.

"I can see why someone might want Jamison dead, if he was trying to get the Wahine's to give up their hotel, but why kill Mrs. Aldrich?"

"That's what we need to find out." I scooted closer to him on the sofa. "April and I are going back to investigate his office after everyone is asleep."

"I'm not sure…"

"We haven't come to any harm yet." I leaned back to see his face. "Has Joe said anything to you about how Mrs. Aldrich actually died? I'm sure he knows."

Ethan sighed. "She was poisoned. He wasn't able to get Manano to tell him what kind of poison, though, so don't ask."

"Is there a storage building close by? Somewhere the Wahine's keep gardening tools?" I'd be willing to bet my favorite red stilettos that there was poison hidden on the grounds. "I bet Mrs. Aldrich found out something she shouldn't." I laid my check on his broad chest.

"You mean she nosed around, asked questions, and went where she didn't belong."

"Most likely."

"Like you."

"Well…I…" He had me there. "I'll be careful, I promise. I have no desire to be locked into a trunk, shot at, or chased through a carnival funhouse ever again. I'm being very low key this time."

He laughed, his chest rumbling under my ear. "Sure, you are."

"Stop." I gave him a playful slap on the arm. "What could possibly go wrong?"

"You really want me to answer that?"

"No." As careful as I planned on being, things did tend to go wrong for me. But, as long as I told Ethan and Joe where I would be, things should be just fine. "What do you want to do until supper?"

"How does a walk on the beach sound? We're on our honeymoon, you know. Can't have you spending all your time with my sister. We could find a secluded spot, watch the wind surfers, and make out."

I stood and held out my hand. "A walk on the beach sounds perfect."

I stood outside our cottage and breathed deep of the salt-and-seaweed laden air. Closing my eyes, I made out the sound of the waves slapping the shore. I still felt warm and fuzzy from necking with my husband. We had decided to forgo supper, staying in our cottage and ordering room service instead. Ethan's love kept me fortified and gave me courage. A warm breeze kissed my face as tenderly as Ethan had minutes before. I almost had second thoughts about leaving him alone for an hour or two.

Footsteps pounding up the walk. I opened my eyes.

"Aunt Eunice, what are you doing here?" My aunt raced toward me, dressed in black, a huge grin on her face.

"I'm here to help you and April. You'll need a lookout. I can blend in when I want to." She rubbed her hands together. "This will be so much fun! Uncle Roy doesn't even know I'm gone."

I peered over her shoulder to where April stood with Uncle Roy coming up behind her like a locomotive. "He does now."

"Eunice, are you out of your mind?" He stopped beside her and crossed his arms.

"Shhh. You'll wake people up, and we'll be found out." She mimicked his body language.

"You are not going anywhere." Even in the dark, I knew my uncle's face was darkening.

"Oh, yes I am." She turned to me. "Let's go. Night's a wasting."

I gave an apologetic glance to my uncle, a heavy kiss on Ethan's lips, then took Aunt Eunice by the hand. "I'll take good care of her."

"Who is going to take care of you?" Uncle Roy sniffed.

"I will." April patted his shoulder.

He nodded. "You're likely the most sensible. I'll be here with Ethan until y'all get back. You have one hour."

And then what? We turn into pumpkins? "April screams at her own shadow." Sensible, my foot.

"You aren't helping your case, sweetheart." Ethan gave me a peck on the forehead. "Y'all three stay together, and you should be all right."

At least my husband had faith in me.

"Where's Joe?" I asked April as we kept to the shadows on our way to the main house.

"Said he had something to do. I think he's doing some investigating on his own."

No way! "We need to solve this case first." Then maybe my bossy cousin would get off my back about me undertaking things too big for me to handle.

"Do you have your tazer?" Aunt Eunice asked.

"Yes, why?"

"I think you should give it to me so I can shock anyone who comes around while you're snooping."

"No, I think I'll keep it." Was she nuts? She'd most likely taze me or April, or herself.

I shoved aside a low hanging branch and peered through a hibiscus plant. No lights glowed in the house. I was pretty sure I remembered the way to the library slash office. Hopefully the door would be unlocked.

The others followed me as I stepped into the opening and dashed across the lawn. Horror! The light over the shuffleboard court highlighted April's blonde hair and Aunt Eunice's grey. What did my red hair look like? We needed to get under cover fast before someone glanced out a window.

I grabbed the doorknob to the front door and pushed. Locked. Aunt Eunice and April barreled into me, knocking the air from my lungs. "Back off!"

"I thought Mr. Wahine said the main house was open to guests at all times." April peered through the glass.

"He did." I leaned against the building. "Did he at any time say anything about hiding a key anywhere?"

"Sure he did. At check-in. Most likely you and Ethan were too wrapped up in each other to pay attention." Aunt Eunice picked up a tropical-colored frog. "There's one in the frog's butt. Isn't that clever?" She handed me the key.

"Very. Thanks." I inserted it in the lock and listened for the satisfying sound of it disengaging. There. I handed the key back to my aunt and led the way inside. "Lock it behind you. It will make it harder to be surprised."

Aunt Eunice turned, knocking into a table, and lunged for a swaying lamp. "Got it!"

"Shh." April and I hissed in unison.

"If you can't be quiet and careful, go back." I shook my head and moved down the hall.

Praise God, the office was unlocked. I slipped inside.

April joined me, leaving Aunt Eunice in the hall. "She said she would recite a bible passage if someone was coming."

Good grief. "Look for anything that might tell us whether Mr. Wahine is involved in shady dealings or had worked with Mr. Jamison."

April moved to the bookshelves while I jiggled desk drawers. They were all locked.

I eyed the laptop and wondered whether it required a password. If it was for guests' use, it shouldn't. I pressed the button and watched as it came to life. "What's Mr. Jamison's first name?"

"I have no idea." April shook a book. "Maybe it's written in the guest book."

"Which is at the front desk." This was a total waste of time.

"Love is patient, love is kind, love is..." Aunt

Eunice's voice drifted loud and clear.

April clutched the book to her chest and plopped on the sofa. I grabbed a book and fell into a wingchair as the door opened.

Leroy Wahine marched in. "Kind of late for reading, isn't it?"

"Is it a problem?" I thought my heart would stop. "Your father said we could visit any time."

"That is correct." He pulled a key from his pocket and opened a drawer to the desk. With a manila folder in his hand, he stopped in the middle of the room. "Why is there an old lady babbling to herself in the hall?"

"That's my senile aunt. Excuse us. I need to care for her." I handed him the book I held and stood, motioning for April to follow.

"Why are all three of you dressed in black?" Leroy frowned. "I don't think you're being entirely truthful with me. I've heard about you, Mrs. Banning."

"From Susan Wood, no doubt."

"Yes. She warned us all about your nosiness." He smiled without humor. "My suggestion to you is for you to enjoy your visit and go home. Nothing more."

That sounded an awful lot like a threat. My hackles rose. I wanted nothing more than to stick my tazer to his bum and wipe that smirk off his face. "I'll keep that in mind, thanks." I turned to April. "Do you have the book you wanted?"

"Yes, thank you." With her nose in the air, she sashayed past our unfriendly host and out the door.

Leroy leaned close. "People are talking about you, Mrs. Banning." He winked and left me standing there gaping like a fish.

What people? I wanted to shout after him. Were they talking about me in a good way or a bad one? Somehow, I guessed it was bad.

I joined April and my aunt in the hall. "Really? Corinthians?"

Aunt Eunice shrugged. "It's the first thing that came to mind. Found out anything?"

"Nothing more than the fact that Leroy Wahine doesn't like me."

"What else is new?" Aunt Eunice grinned. "I'm hungry. Let's go to your cottage and grab something to eat."

"What do you mean? I'm likeable. Everybody likes me." Seriously. "If everybody liked you, someone wouldn't be trying to kill you."

14

Aunt Eunice's words haunted me into the morning hours. The only person on the island I could truthfully say didn't care for me would be Susan Woods. I had no idea why. Just because she had read a few newspaper articles about my crime solving wasn't enough motivation. Not in my book, anyway.

I sat up in bed and slid my legs over the side. It was hard to believe today was our fifth day on the island and I was neck-deep in two murders. Depressing, really. Not only because two people were dead, but also because all I knew in that five day's time was the possibility that Mr. Jamison might have wanted to take control of the land the Wahine Bed and Breakfast sat on.

Ethan rolled over. "Can't sleep?"

"No." I pushed aside a curl that had fallen over his eyes. "What do you want to do today?"

"Parasailing?" He raised his eyebrows.

The thought scared me spitless, but I'd try anything once. "Sure. Do you think we can escape without the others?"

He grinned. "We can sure try. Might have a better chance if we grab breakfast in Lahaina."

"I'll get dressed." I jumped to my feet and dashed into the bathroom.

I reached for a sundress. No, not if I was going to be floating over people's heads. I opted instead for white capris and a royal blue tank top with sequins. I'd look like part of the sky. After tying my hair back into a ponytail and grabbing the camera, I rejoined Ethan and hand-in-hand we headed to the front of the hotel to see about renting a car for the day, which would leave the rental van for the others.

Joy bubbled inside. I was ridiculously excited about spending an entire day with my new husband. Just me, him, and the island of Maui. What could be better?

My aunt and uncle turned the corner. I clutched Ethan's arm. "We need to hurry."

A young man handed him the keys to a candy-apple red convertible. Perfect! Ethan handed him a ten dollar bill and slid behind the wheel. I rushed to the passenger side and climbed in. Made it by the skin of our teeth.

"Yoo hoo!" Aunt Eunice waved.

I waved back, then slid what I called my Hollywood sunglasses over my eyes. "See you later! Enjoy your day." I leaned in to Ethan. "Floor it." I felt awful for ditching them, but Ethan and I deserved a day to ourselves, didn't we? I never should have called April after someone threw the spear at us. The rental car roared down the road.

"What's wrong?" Ethan reached over and grasped my hand.

"It hasn't been the honeymoon you envisioned, has it?"

"What do you mean?" He glanced at me. "Any

day with you is a honeymoon." His mouth quirked. "Besides, how many guys can say they helped solve a murder on their honeymoon?"

"Don't tease." I faced out the passenger side of the car.

The wind whipped my hair and kissed my skin with the scent of Hawaii. Maybe I would ditch my ailing Sonata for a Mustang convertible when we got home. The candy store was making good money. Somehow I doubted Ethan would argue too much. He looked perfectly happy behind the wheel.

He smiled. "I'm not teasing. Anywhere, any time with you, is paradise."

How did I warrant such a splendid gift from God?

"I love you." I pressed my lips against his neck.

"I love you, but if you really want to go parasailing, you might want to stop nuzzling my neck."

"Do I get to pick which I'd rather do?" I ran my fingers through his hair. "Because it isn't a difficult decision."

He flicked a glance at me. "We don't have to go. There are plenty of other things to do."

"I want to." Actually, I knew how much he wanted to, and didn't have the heart to tell him how much the idea scared me.

Settling back into my seat, I watched the deep greens and blues of the landscape whip past. A luxury cruise ship perched on the ocean like a whale. A smaller boat carried passengers to shore. Tourists anxious to explore Maui's treasures. How many of them would run across a murder or two while here? Not many, I'd guess.

I wouldn't think of those things today. I grabbed

Ethan's hand and gave him a shaky smile.

"Don't worry, Tink," he said. "If you decide you don't want to parasail once we get on the boat, it won't be too late to change your mind. But remember, fairies fly."

"Very funny." Even his endearing nickname for me couldn't alleviate my nervousness. I sent a prayer heavenward and tried to convince myself that floating above the earth, tied to a nylon rope, would only bring me closer to God.

Ethan stopped the car on a gravel drive and flashed his teeth. "Ready?"

"You bet!" If faking enthusiasm kept that grin on his face, then so be it. We'd had anything but a model honeymoon so far.

He helped me from the car and practically ran toward the boat guy. "Reservation for Banning."

"Yes, sir. Climb aboard. My name's Paul and that young whipper-snapper over there is Junior."

My stomach churned as I allowed Paul to help me onboard. Instead I tried to focus on how dark his skin was. He looked Caucasian, but his skin was browned to the shade of a walnut. If Junior's skin was any indication, he was trying to catch up to his senior. Blue eyes sparkled out of both faces and I'm pretty sure their white smiles were intended to calm me. It didn't work.

Taking a deep breath, I sat in the middle seat and remained as still as possible. What if I got seasick? Or airsick? What if I passed out while in the sky? I clutched my stomach.

This was ridiculous! I had stared down people pointing a gun at me. Surely I could handle this.

Once Ethan sat next to me, Paul gunned the

engine, and we bounced across the water's surface. I figured we cruised half mile off shore before Paul slowed and turned to me. "Ladies first?"

I shook my head hard enough for pieces of hair to come loose from my ponytail.

Ethan laughed and stood. "I'm ready."

Paul and Junior strapped him into the harness and instructed Ethan to stand on a small platform at the rear of the boat. "We're going to let the wind carry you out and then in twenty minutes we'll reel you in like a fish." Paul smacked Ethan on the chest. "Ready?"

"Yep." Ethan winked in my direction, gave a thumbs up as the boat roared forward, and then sailed into the sky.

I couldn't help but grin along with him. Soon, he was nothing but a speck in the sky. My palms sweated. It would be the fastest twenty minutes of my life, followed by the longest.

Remembering I'd slung the camera around my neck before leaving our cottage, I zoomed in on Ethan's rapturous expression and snapped a few photos. Thank the good Lord for a good camera with a twenty-five times zoom lens. I'd be able to get some great shots.

Way too soon, Paul and Junior reeled Ethan back to the boat and strapped me into the harness. I closed my eyes and shrieked when the boat increased speed.

"You'll love it!" Ethan shouted.

I shook my head and felt my feet leave the boat. Help me, God. Help me. I gripped the ropes on each side of my head. My knuckles ached. I opened my eyes and gasped.

The ocean was so far below. So blue. To my left

rose the buildings of Lahaina. To my right, a small island. Below me, lots and lots of boats. The scene was truly idyllic.

Wrapping my arms around the ropes, I lifted the camera to my eye and zoomed in on Lahaina's main street. Expressions were hard to see, but people dotted the sidewalks and cafes. Families strolled along the shore. I stopped on a familiar face. "Aunt Eunice!" I waved and followed her progress down the street.

Why did she look as if she were sneaking up on someone? I moved the camera a ways in front of her. Susan Wood and Manano sat side-by-side at a table in the shadows. At least, I thought it was them. No way to be completely sure, but whoever it was looked mighty cozy and didn't seem worried that someone would see them. I scanned the shore with the camera, which was proving to be every bit as good as binoculars.

I leaned forward. Was that the Wahine siblings waving their arms at each other? It looked as if they were arguing. Oh, I wished Paul would lower me just a bit so I could see and hear better. I snapped a few photos and lowered the camera.

Oh! I froze.

Someone should have told me that leaning forward while parasailing could result in the world's worst case of vertigo. For a while, I'd forgotten to be afraid, now the feeling rushed back like a tsunami, stealing my breath and causing the blood to rush to my feet.

Not a moment too soon, the rope tugged and I lowered, much too slowly, back to the boat and into Ethan's arms. I took deep breaths and rested my head against his strong chest. "I survived."

"Were you really that frightened?"

"Not for a while. I was busy taking pictures of suspicious activity, but once I realized how far up I was—let's just say, I don't want to do that particular activity again."

His chest rumbled. "We'll snorkel Molokai tomorrow, okay? That ought to be tame enough for you."

"Maybe, but the papers we got with our rented gear said there were barricudas and sharks."

15

I sipped my pineapple drink and watched as Ethan body-surfed. Having recovered from my parasailing ordeal, I wanted nothing more than to enjoy the late afternoon with a yummy drink and the company of my family. Especially since I had oodles of questions for my aunt.

"I saw you in Lahaina today." I peered at her over my sunglasses.

"I saw you and Ethan ditching us this morning." She raised her eyebrows.

"Well, I, uh…"

"It's your honeymoon, I know." She reached over and patted my arm. "Don't worry. I'm glad you didn't say anything in Lahaina. You would have blown my cover. While you were off playing, I was being a detective."

"What did you find out?" I turned on my side and took a long draw from my straw. "Through my camera lens it looked like you were spying on Susan and Manano. Is that right?"

She frowned. "Where were you?"

"In the sky."

"Fine, don't tell me." She shrugged. "April and

Joe ditched me, too. Roy wasn't feeling well, so—"

"You went investigating on your own?" That straightened me up. "Do you realize how dangerous that is?"

"Like you don't do it all the time." She waved a hand at me. "Anyway, I took a shuttle to Lahaina to do some shopping and saw our little lovebirds—"

"Susan and Manano, right?" I sat up and shoved my toes in the sand.

"Would you stop asking that? You sound like a broken record. Yes, it was them." Aunt Eunice exhaled sharply and shook her head. "Anyway, they were arguing—"

"Like Leroy and Camilla Wahine."

"I don't know about them, but." She gave me a stern look. "Susan was upset because our dear police officer hadn't taken care of some kind of 'business'" She made finger quotes in the air. "And that 'she' whoever that is, but I have my guess, was still nosing around."

Hmmm, sounded sinister, and I could lay money down on who 'she' was. "I could see the dear brother and sister arguing, too, or at least that's what it looked like." What could possibly have everyone in an uproar?

"Howdy." April plopped into a chair next to me. "Guess what I found out?"

Aunt Eunice peered around me. "That it's rude to disappear from the people who paid for your vacation?"

Her face reddened. "Sorry about that, but Joe wanted to spend some time together."

"We're your chaperones. Y'all aren't married yet." Aunt Eunice crossed her arms and settled back.

"Never mind her," I said. "Spill your guts."

"Jamison's first name is Bob, or Robert, rather. He owned Jamison's Resort Construction. Guess who is his partners?"

"Susan Wood is one."

"Bingo!"

"Who is the other?" My straw made slurping sounds on the bottom of my empty glass. I glanced behind us for a server. The Wahine might be a bed and breakfast, but they treated the guests as if it were a resort. Pure paradise, when people weren't dying anyway.

"It's a corporation. Plumeria Builders, based in Honolulu." She sure looked proud of herself.

"More drinks?" Camille stepped beside us, pretty in a fuschia flowered dress.

"Please. Pineapple Mango all around." I waved my hand with a flourish. We were finally getting somewhere with the case. It all centered around Jamison's business and the Wahine's being desperate for money.

Of course, you couldn't tell by our surroundings. The grounds were immaculate, the service impeccable, and the rooms top-of-the-line. Something smelled rank in this tropical oasis. I reclined back in the lounger. Yep, we were going to solve this mystery same as the previous three. I knew it. I just needed to dig deeper into Jamison's background.

Ethan waved from the water, looking every bit as fine as a cover model for some risqué woman's magazine. With the sun highlighting his blond hair and bronzed muscles, his bathing suit riding low on his hips, I almost tossed caution to the wind, forgetting my best friend and aunt sat beside me. I wanted to run to him, throw my legs around his waist and tumble into the surf. My breath quickened. Mercy!

"Earth to Summer." April wiggled her fingers in front of my face.

"Huh?"

"Where are you?" Her brow furrowed, then her gaze followed mine and she grinned. "Never mind. I think I know."

My face heated. "I'm thinking of the goings on at Wahine's B & B." We stopped talking for a moment while our drinks were delivered.

"Sure you are." She sipped her drink. "Oh, good. Here comes Joe. Maybe he has some news for us."

Joe bent to kiss her then perched at the foot of her lounger. "Good news, ladies." He waggled his eyebrows.

If Ethan weren't strutting toward me, sparkling with water drops, I might be able to concentrate. My beloved broke the spell when he shook his hair off on me. I shrieked and swatted at him.

"What did you find out?" He plopped beside me, almost toppling me into the sand. Sometimes my gallant knight was anything but.

"Well," Joe said. "I contacted a buddy of mine on the LAPD. Seems our friend Jamison has been on their radar for quite a while on suspicions of lending money in less than reputable means."

"A loan shark?" I straightened.

"Possibly, although there isn't yet sufficient evidence to convict him."

"Impossible to convict a dead person," Aunt Eunice stated. "But I'm thinking it's time to get cozy with the Mrs."

"Wahine?" Why didn't I think of her? The quiet woman stayed in the background of her husband's stronger personality. Everyone knew still waters ran deep. She probably knew everything about everyone. "I think that's a great idea, but I'll have to go with you. It's too dangerous."

Ethan snorted.

"What?"

"We've been telling you that for over a year. Now, when it's your aunt doing the sleuthing, it's another story."

"Well, of course it is." What did he think? That I would let a sixty-year-old woman confront a possible criminal alone?

Aunt Eunice shook her head. "I think I should do this alone. Mrs. Wahine is around my age and won't suspect anything." She nodded. "Yep, I'll talk to her tomorrow when she's puttering in her flower garden. She does that every morning."

My aunt was more observant than I ever thought. Pride rose in me. Ever since I'd needed her help in solving the murder at the county fair, she had been itching to get involved again. "Okay. But we have to know where you are at all times." Uncle Roy was going to kill me.

"Stop!"

I swiveled to look behind me.

Susan ran, high heels in one hand, the other holding a floppy hat to her head, after a little wire-haired dog. "Somebody stop that animal. It stole my mail."

Ethan, ever the hero, dashed to the rescue and tackled the fiend to the ground. The dog rewarded him with the mail and dog kisses.

"Thank you so much." Susan grabbed what looked like a bill and an invitation from Ethan's hand. "I plan on extending my stay on Maui, so had my mail forwarded here. I have no idea where this monster came from."

"He's a sweetie." I kneeled beside the dog and searched for an ID tag. No collar. "I wish I could take you home, sweetie. Truly would love you." Maybe. My Cairn was fickle when it came to strange animals.

"Rambo!" Leroy Wahine jogged down the beach. "Sorry. He tends to get loose once in a while. He's harmless."

Rambo? I stifled a grin and stood. "No harm done."

"Easy for you to say." Susan huffed and whirled to make her way back to the hotel.

"Aloha." Leroy picked up his dog and headed back the way he had arrived.

The beach sure was busy. I grabbed my towel from the back of my chair. "I'm heading up to shower before supper."

As I turned to leave, a caught a glimpse of something white under the green of a hibiscus bush.

16

After glancing around to see whether anyone was paying attention to me. Of course Ethan was. I grabbed the envelope and read Susan's name. I smiled and waved at my husband and continued my trek to the cottage. It wouldn't do to let him know it was Susan's. Especially not after the ruckus she caused with the dog.

I was knee-deep in a murder investigation. I'd check out the contents of the envelope and return it to her myself.

No sooner had I closed the door behind me than I was reaching for a steak knife left from a previous supper. Unfortunately, it wasn't the first envelope I'd slit open with the hopes of sealing closed with no one the wiser. I slid the blade under the flap and voila! A single sheet of paper fell out.

Written in bold letters was the words PAY UP OR SUFFER JAMISON'S FATE.

I folded onto the sofa. What was Susan mixed up in? If Jamison was suspected of being a loan shark, who could he have angered enough to kill him, and why would they be threatening Susan?

Every answer I uncovered raised a handful of

more questions. Why was Susan on Maui? Why was she consistently seen in Manano's company? Was she friend or foe? I shook my head, wishing I had never gotten involved. After someone threw the spear, Ethan and I should have packed our things and gone to a different island.

I released the note, letting it flutter to the beige carpet like a wounded butterfly. I couldn't walk away now. Maybe God sent us here to save someone from suffering Jamison's and Mrs. Aldrich's fate. I needed to talk to the dead woman's husband. Had he left the island yet?

After changing from my bathing suit to walking shorts and a tank top, I left Ethan a note letting him know where I was going, put Susan's mail in the top dresser drawer, and then locked the cottage behind me.

The Aldrich cottage wasn't far from mine and Ethan's, and the front door stood open. "Hello? Mr. Aldrich?"

"Back here."

I followed his voice to the bedroom. An open suitcase sat on the bed.

Mr. Aldrich tossed clothing inside, leaving his wife's in a pile on the floor. "What do you want?"

Not his usual friendly self, but I understood, under the circumstances. "Is there anything I can do for you? When are you leaving?"

He sighed. "Tonight was the earliest flight I could take. They'll ship my wife's body, once they're finished with the investigation." He sagged onto the bed. "Outside of bringing her back, there isn't anything anyone can do."

"I can pray."

He huffed. "That won't bring her back. My wife was the one with the faith."

"Mr. Aldrich." I laid a hand on his shoulder. "Do you know why anyone would want to kill her?"

"Sure, I do. She started asking questions about Jamison's death." He shook his head. "Always fancied herself an older Nancy Drew. I called her my Agatha." He brushed his hand across his face. "Like you, I guess."

Except I was still alive. I heard the accusation in his voice. "I'm sorry."

"Guess you want to know if she found out anything." He stood and moved to the dresser and took a cigar box out of the top drawer. "She kept all her notes in here."

"Did y'all come to Maui to follow Jamison? Your wife said it was your anniversary."

"It was our anniversary." He slapped the suitcase closed. "She wanted to solve a mystery in celebration. Said the love between a man and a woman was the second greatest mystery outside of God's love for us." He fixed his eyes on me. "You solve this thing for her, you hear?"

"Yes, sir." Tears stung my eyes as I accepted the box. "I'll do my best."

"No." He shook me. "You do this. You stay alive and found out who killed her."

"Summer?" Ethan stepped beside me. "Everything all right here?"

"Yes." I held out my hand to Mr. Aldrich. "Have a safe trip. May God go with you."

He grunted, grabbed his case, and marched out.

I turned and buried my face in Ethan's chest, letting the tears escape.

"Hey, baby." He cradled me close. "Are you okay? Did he hurt you?"

I shook my head. "No, I'm just hurting for him." I lifted my face. "I promised him I would find out who killed his wife."

"Sure you did." He smiled. "I wouldn't expect anything less." Keeping his arm around my shoulder, he led me back to our cottage.

"Into bed for you. I'll bring back supper." Ethan pulled down the bedcovers.

"I'm not sleepy. It's only six o'clock."

"Then look through the box in your hand, but I want you resting in bed in your pajamas. I know you won't go wandering around in your nightie."

True. I smiled through my tears and nodded. "I will stay here. Let the family know I have a headache and we won't be accepting visitors."

"I will." He kissed me. "Be back in a flash."

After slipping into my nightgown, I crawled into bed and scooted against the headboard. The box sat next to me, chanting my name. I opened the lid then closed it.

Mr. Aldrich's grief spilled over onto me, dispelling my previous curiosity about his wife's notes. I loved solving mysteries, but didn't relish dying for it. I leaned my head back, knocking it against the headboard. That would leave a bruise.

With my finger, I traced the ornate, upraised design on the box. One corner was smashed and smudged as if the box had been thrown. I shrugged. Maybe Mrs. Aldrich retrieved it from the garbage. It was a pretty, sturdy thing with its forest green and gold designs. I sighed and pushed off the bed.

Lying around would get me nowhere. The cottage

didn't have a television, and since I was in my nightie, I couldn't go borrow a book. I parted the curtains and stared out into the beginning dusk.

The sunsets on Maui were indescribable and usually lifted my spirits. Suddenly, I yearned for the Ozark mountains of home. The peacefulness of Mountain Springs.

Somebody walked down the beach, a man, from the body build, and sat on the sand. The glow from an ember shined in his hand. I let the curtains fall, allowing the man his solitary smoke. On second thought…

I changed into capri sweats and a long-sleeved tee-shirt. A walk on the beach might be just the thing I needed to clear my head and lift my mood. I left a note for Ethan, promising not to go far, and slipped my feet into flip-flops. Already I felt better in anticipation of feeling the waves on my feet.

The smoker was gone when I stepped outside, and I practically skipped to the water. I sat in the sand, arms wrapped around my bent knees and gave up my cares to God. After all, He was the only one strong enough to make sure I solved this mystery without joining Him any time soon. If He chose to call me home, then so be it, but I would do my best to find Mrs. Aldrich's and Jamison's killer as promised.

I stood and moved into the water, wading until it crested my knees. Warm silk caressed my skin. I stretched out my arms and lifted my face to heaven. Thank you, God, for a place such as this. Other than my beloved mountains, this was paradise.

Footsteps pounded behind me. I turned. Someone barreled into me, taking me into the dark sea.

Holding my breath, I flailed at the hands holding

me under. He was going to drown me!

Think, Summer!

I doubled up my fist and hit him where it counted. No time for modesty. For good measure, I grabbed his crotch and pulled up. He sagged, and I fought my way free. Before I could get my feet firmly under me, he was staggering from the water.

"Hey!" I splashed after him. "Come back and fight like a man!" I giggled as adrenaline coursed through my body. I hated how my emotions betrayed me in a life or death situation. I either laughed or cried. I guess this time I was a comedian.

On the sand, my attacker stumbled away, leaving me to collapse. I thanked God for the self-defense classes Ethan had badgered me to take. I wouldn't have known that grabbing a handful of private parts and tugging could be so effective.

My chest heaved as my lungs struggled to draw in air. I tried to remember any distinguishing features of the man, but came up with nothing but long pants, strong hands, and most likely a bruised ego. So much for a relaxing sit at the ocean's side.

I pushed to my feet and made my way back to the cottage, thankful Ethan hadn't returned home yet. My steps faltered. Why hadn't he? He had said he was bringing dinner back.

I rushed inside and searched for my cell phone. Within seconds, I held my breath as it rang on the other end.

"Sorry, Babe. I got tied up talking to Joe."

I released my pent up breathe at the sound of his voice. "I was worried."

"I'm fine. I thought you were resting."

"Couldn't sleep, so I took a short walk on the

beach." I grimaced. Probably shouldn't have said that.

He sighed. "I wish you wouldn't do that."

"What are you and Joe talking about?" I plopped into a chair.

"Jamison. Seems the guy was mixed up in some pretty bad stuff. Did a lot of people wrong. He wasn't the actual shark in the loaning operation, but rather a middle man who stiffed the boss."

"How does this affect anyone here?"

"That's what we need to find out."

The plot thickened. I eyed the cigar box on the bed. Soon, I would have to dig through a dead woman's thoughts and see whether she had found anything to help us.

17

"I am leaving on the next flight out of here!" Maryann Franklin tossed her fork to her plate with a clatter and stormed from the dining room.

Bruce leaped from his chair and bolted after her.

My hand paused with its bite of roll clutched in my fist. Should I follow?

Although the two were on my list of suspects, they stayed to themselves most of the time. Out of sight, out of mind, so they say. Before anyone could stop me, I shoved the last of my breakfast into my mouth and mumbled, "I'm going to make sure she's okay," before running out of the room.

"Summer."

I glanced over my shoulder at Ethan, motioned my head for him to follow, and kept running. When the Franklins stopped suddenly, I did, too, and ducked behind a fake potted tree.

"I see you, Mrs. Banning." Maryann rolled her eyes. "It's no secret that Bruce and I have fought our entire sham of a honeymoon." She took a deep shuddering breath.

"Can I help?" I stepped from my ridiculous hiding place.

"Not unless you can find the five thousand dollars my dear husband invested in a dead man!" She whirled and marched outside.

"Are you talking about Mr. Jamison?" I kicked off my flip flops, bent to retrieve them, and rushed after her.

"Yes." She stopped fast enough for me to run into her. "His investment idea sounded wonderful, at first." She dropped to a stone bench. "Five thousand dollars for a timeshare property on Maui." She waved her arm. "Does this look like time share property to you?"

"The bed and breakfast?"

"Yes. Oh, Bruce will be so angry with me." Sighing, she covered her face. "Mr. Jamison stiffed a lot of people. Us included."

Ethan and Bruce joined us. Bruce sat beside his wife.

"Did y'all kill him?" I didn't see any reason to beat around the bush.

"Of course not." Bruce glowered. "Are you two seriously the only guests here that are not involved in this ridiculous scam?"

"Apparently so." Ethan rubbed his chin then glanced toward the dining room. "At least most of us."

What did that mean? I felt as if I were living an Agatha Christie story where the characters were knocked off one-by-one. "Has anyone called the police?"

"Isn't Manano a cop?" Bruce smirked. "A poor excuse for one, anyway. This weekend was supposed to be a gathering of interested parties to determine who stayed when. The whole thing was a joke."

I didn't think timeshares worked that way, but what did I know? "Is that why you tried to kill yourself, Maryann?"

She shrugged. "We've lost everything. With Jamison dead, there's no collecting now. Seems the dearly departed Jamison had no timeshare. He swindled people out of money in order to build some resort somewhere."

"What do the Wahines say?"

"They're innocent." Bruce raked his fingers through his hair. "Had no idea any of this was going on. They just thought they were having a really productive week." He stood and held out his hand. "Come on, Maryann. Going home is a great idea."

Color me confused. I took their vacant seat and patted the bench for Ethan to join me. "What do you make of all this?"

"Sounds like we have a hotel full of people with a motive. Including your uncle."

"What?" I jerked to face him.

"Your uncle said he came not only because you were in trouble, but because he wanted to check on a possible investment. I think this is the investment."

My stomach sank. Surely Uncle Roy didn't pay a chunk of money for a time share. What about his retirement? "Uncle Roy wouldn't kill anyone."

"No, I know he wouldn't, but I think Roy needs to answer some questions."

We waited until the others exited the dining room and fell into step beside them. Instead of branching off to our own cottage, Ethan and I followed them into theirs.

"Roy, we need to talk." Ethan waved him to a chair.

"Yep, I'm guessing we do." Uncle Roy ran his hands down the legs of his pants. "Have a seat, Eunice. You ain't going to be happy about this."

Her eyes bugged, but she did as she was told. "What did you do now?"

Ethan held up his hand. "Roy, what type of investment did you come to Maui for? We know it wasn't only to check on Summer, you told us yourself."

"I thought I could get a timeshare for me and the missus. Thought it would be nice to spend a month or so here every year." Uncle Roy rested his elbows on his knees and leaned forward. "Thank the good Lord I didn't fork over any money. Told the fella I wasn't going to until I'd taken a look for myself. He wasn't happy, but he agreed."

"I'm thinking you're right." I sagged onto the sofa. Thank goodness my uncle had a level head. Things could have ended very differently for my family.

"Well, that don't make me mad," Aunt Eunice said. "I knew all about it. Found the emails one day on the computer. Knew it sounded too good to be true."

"This puts you toward the top of the suspect list, if Manano finds out." Joe shook his head. "Especially after Aunt Eunice chatted up Mrs. Aldrich, and she turned up dead."

"I know. We're in a pickle for sure." Uncle Roy lifted his head. "Why do you think I haven't said anything? I hoped by keeping my mouth shut, nobody would know of my involvement. I'm a shade embarrassed."

"We might still be able to keep your name out of

this." Joe crossed his arms and leaned against the wall. "It ought to be easy enough to keep Manano's suspicions on Summer. The man isn't the brightest pebble on the beach, and since my cousin can't keep her nose out of trouble, she ought to cause enough upheaval for Manano to focus on her."

The spider web continued to wind around, in and out, until I had no idea which end was up. The only thing I knew for sure was that folks involved in a false timeshare offer were turning up dead, and I didn't want my uncle to be one of them.

"Unless Jamison had a list somewhere." I chewed my nail. "He must have. Then, whoever killed him, is going down the list, getting rid of witnesses."

"What if Manano has it?" April moved to stand next to Joe. "Or the killer?"

"We need to find it." I glanced around the room at all the faces I loved, and prayed my passion for solving mysteries wouldn't get any of them killed.

"You're crazy." Joe pushed away from the wall. "Manano has Jamison's laptop. If there's a list, it's on there and you won't have access to it." He marched to the kitchen and opened the small refrigerator. "Why isn't there any soda?"

"Probably because you drank it all?" I shook my head. "Maybe Jamison had a partner? I doubt the man was scamming people on his own. It seems like a large undertaking."

Joe straightened. "That's the smartest thing you've said in a long time."

"Which part?" I frowned.

Ethan leaned to whisper in my ear. "I think he means the part about a partner."

"A partner killing people." Tingles shot up my

spine faster than a rocket. I pushed him away so I could concentrate. "Stop whispering. It tickles."

"That's the idea." He chuckled.

"You two lovebirds stop nuzzling," Aunt Eunice scolded. "We have work to do."

"And managed to get way off track." Joe slammed the fridge. "We need to find another victim."

"Alive, I hope. I'll be right back." I left and retrieved Susan's mail, returning minutes later. "I found this under a bush earlier when a dog had Susan Woods's mail. It's a threat." I handed it to Joe. "Maybe I should go talk to her."

"Maybe Ethan should." April giggled. "The woman seems to like him better."

No way on earth would I let my husband be alone with her. Not for one little bit.

Ethan winked. "I think I'm up to the challenge."

"No, you're not." I punched his arm. "Unless I go with you."

"How about Ethan and I go?" Joe moved back to April's side. "She definitely seems to relate more to men."

"But then I won't know what's going on!"

"We'll tell you."

My nail went back in my mouth. "No, it needs to be somewhere I can eavesdrop. Something always gets left out when information is passed along secondhand."

"I'm a cop, Summer." Joe crossed his arms. "I think I can properly relay information."

"Still." There had to be a way. I rarely saw her at the meals, and occasionally on the beach. "We need to find out where she's going tomorrow and follow her."

"And how, Sherlock, do you propose we do that?" Joe smirked.

"We ask the Wahine's if she's rented a car or asked directions." I grinned. "I'll do it first thing in the morning. Then, we follow her. You two sashay up and start a conversation, while I pretend to be somewhere else mentally, and—"

Joe guffawed. "That shouldn't be hard for you."

I glared. "I will stay a few steps away and be engrossed in the scenery while actually listening to y'all. It's a brilliant plan." I dared any of them to disagree.

"I know where she's going," Aunt Eunice said, grinning like the Cheshire cat. "I heard that boy, David, ask her if she wanted to visit the seven pools. They're taking the road to Hana." That twisting, turning, hundred miles of one-lane road.

I couldn't help but remember the last road we were on. The one where somebody tried to run me over.

18

"I want Ethan to drive." I set the tour pamphlet on the hood of the van and stabbed at it with my index finger. "This says we should pick our best driver." Not only that, but the warning of 600+ turns had me popping motion sickness pills and praying I could convince Joe to let me sit in the front seat.

"I haven't driven the group this whole trip." Uncle Roy crossed his arms.

"And you aren't doing it today. Not on this road." I plucked the keys from his hands and handed them to Ethan.

A few cars over, Susan climbed into a convertible with David Hatcher. If we didn't leave right when they did, we might not see them again until they returned later that evening. "I'm sitting up front, unless y'all want me to get sick all over you, and we need to leave now."

Everyone climbed into the van, and we pulled from the parking lot mere seconds after Susan. I really hoped they planned on sightseeing. According to the brochure, there were more things to see in a day along the road to Hana than there was time for. I grabbed the pamphlet from the hood and climbed into the front passenger seat, spreading the glossy brochure across my lap.

"Take Highway 36. It turns into 360."

"What if Susan turns off?" Ethan sped up to get closer to her. "Do I turn or continue?"

"We do what she does."

"Won't she know we're following her?" April asked from the middle row of seats.

I shrugged. "Just about everyone who comes to Maui takes this road and there're places to stop everywhere. We won't have to say anything. She doesn't own the island." I dug in my purse and located the Dramamine. "I suggest everyone take one of these."

Joe grabbed the box and handed it around. "I'd like to come back to Hawaii someday, when I'm not trying to find a murderer or having to follow someone else's schedule."

I knew exactly how he felt. Being on my honeymoon and following someone who might intend me harm, was not my idea of a romantic getaway. I rested my hand on Ethan's thigh. At least we were spending time together.

Almost immediately, the scenery took my breath away. Highway 360 was a cliff road, winding around a turquoise ocean. I wished we could have rented a convertible so I could hear the waves. Instead, I closed my eyes for a second, leaned my head back, and pretended.

"She's stopping." Ethan pulled the van over.

I opened my eyes to see mile marker six, then scanned the brochure. Oh, a bamboo forest. I scrambled from the van, grabbing my camera, and stepped aside while the others exited. Susan and

David had already disappeared down a dirt path, and I was anxious to follow. "Aunt Eunice, can you hand me my backpack? The guide says to wear good shoes and bring water."

"Do you have enough for everyone?" She tossed the bag to me.

"One for each."

"I'll wear it." Ethan snatched the pack and slung it over his shoulders. "Let's see what we can find." He grabbed my hand and dragged me into something magical.

A mile from where we parked, we entered into a towering forest of bamboo. The breeze caused the stalks to brush against each other and whisper sweet nothings. At least, that's what I imagined they said. I almost felt as if they called my name and tried to lure me into a fantasy. Sunlight dappled and winked through the swaying stalks. Before too long, our conversation became hushed, almost reverent. I imagined all types of things waiting for us around the bend, such as deranged killers, zombies, Susan and David in an embrace. I wasn't sure which frightened me more.

Hushed words caused me to stop, halting Ethan, and I held up my hand for the others. I held a finger to my mouth and strained to hear. As carefully as possible, I parted the stalks and peered through.

"This is getting out of control." Susan paced the path, waving her arms around as if a swarm of flies plagued her. "Because of one stupid decision, we're all going down, unless we stop her from snooping around. I cannot have everything I've worked for taken from me."

David held out his hands. "Settle down. It's being

taken care of. I promise."

"That's what you keep saying, but she's still a thorn in my side!"

Mercy. Susan really wanted me out of the picture. My mouth dried up. I let the stalks fall back into place and sidled up to Ethan. "I think she's going to have me killed."

He hugged me against him and kissed the top of my head. "I won't let that happen."

"You might not be able to prevent it." I straightened. "Let's go, y'all. No need to be secret now. I've heard all I need to." At least for the time being.

A cloud passed over the sun. No matter how many crimes I tried to solve by snooping where I shouldn't, it never ceased to amaze me that people might actually want me dead. After my prior experiences, what would they try on the island of Maui?

Drench me in blood for the sharks and barracudas? Leave me stranded in the middle of the ocean in a life raft with a slow leak? I shook my head, trying to stop my overactive imagination. I wanted to enjoy my honeymoon, not worry about what waited around the next bend.

We continued our hike through the bamboo forest. The beauty and awe of the place did a lot for raising my spirits. God truly shined when he made these islands.

When we reached the van, Ethan helped me inside and then moved to get behind the wheel. A car careened around the corner. Ethan flattened himself against the door until the reckless driver disappeared around the next corner.

From the tic in his jaw when he got in the van, I could tell Ethan struggled to control his temper. Not many things riled him, but when they did my gentle man turned into a tiger. I'm guessing almost getting hit by a car, after I told him someone wanted to kill me, might have lit his fuse.

Without speaking, he turned the key in the ignition and pulled back onto the road. The scenery left nothing to be desired. The atmosphere inside the van did. No one talked. Everyone stared silently out the window.

It was all my fault. Hawaii was a place to be enjoyed, and me being involved in another mystery spoiled it for everyone. "I'm sorry, guys." I laid a hand on Ethan's arm. "I want to go home."

"We'll be back at the hotel in a few hours." He didn't take his eyes off the road.

"No. I mean *home*."

He glanced out of the corner of his eye. "Nope. Not yet. Not until we get to the bottom of all this. We showed up on our honeymoon, someone dies, and you're left a warning note without us doing anything to get involved."

"We don't plan on going anywhere," Uncle Roy said. "Do we, Eunice?"

Joe sighed. "We'll be staying, too."

"Don't sound so thrilled." The day's gloom blew away on a tropical breeze. My family cared enough to help me. Even Joe. He might sigh and groan, but he wanted to know how this all ended as well as I did. The cop in him wouldn't let him walk away before the end of the story. "So, how do we hurry this thing along? Ethan and I head home soon."

"We keep you visible." Joe straightened. "Not

alone, but out where you can be seen. We drop hints that you know more than you've said. We—watch out!"

Ethan swerved, taking the van up a steep incline, which considering the other side of the road led off a cliff, seemed the best choice. He hit the brakes and cut the ignition.

Ahead of us, a red convertible hung halfway off the same cliff I feared we'd drive off. First, the car appeared to have smashed into the side of a hill, then according to tire marks, skidded toward the cliff. I didn't know what kept it from diving into the ocean, only that I prayed it would stay where it was.

"Ethan, there's still someone in the car." I clutched his arm, knowing without him saying a word that he and Joe would attempt to rescue the person.

With the imminent danger, the surf sounded louder, menacing, an angry god waiting for sacrifice. I closed my eyes and prayed: For their safety and for the unknown person in the car.

"Stay here," he told me.

I never would understand why he kept telling me things he knew I couldn't do. As soon as he scooted from the van, I did the same and was followed by Aunt Eunice and April. We stood on the side of the road and held hands while Ethan and Joe approached the other vehicle. Aunt Eunice's lips moved in silent prayer. I uttered my own, pleading with God not to allow the car to fall.

Ethan and Joe both shook their heads, Ethan pressing numbers on his phone, clearly not knowing how to proceed without backup. The person in the car hadn't moved. Were they alive?

"Check for a pulse!" Seemed a logical thing to

do.

"I will," Joe answered. "Once I can figure out how to without me and the car going over." He stepped closer. "Sir? Can you hear me?"

"Wait." Ethan held out a hand. "That's Franklin, one of the guests at the B & B."

Where was Maryann? I released Aunt Eunice's and Alice's hands and scoured the thick foliage on the side of the road. There! A flash of bright yellow and blue. "Ethan! Joe!"

I knelt beside Maryann's body and felt her neck for a pulse. I found one. A purple goose egg rose above her eyebrow and the right side of her face was scraped. It looked like she might have been thrown from the car when it collided with the hill.

Ethan joined me. "Ambulance is on its way, but it'll be a while. I don't think Franklin's alive. Joe wouldn't let me get too close, but his neck is sitting at an odd angle. The car's ready to go any moment."

"She's got a nasty bump on her head. Do you think it's safe to move her to the seat of the van?" Anything to get her out of the dirt and somewhere more comfortable. She'd feel horrible enough to know Bruce was dead after they'd so recently argued.

"I think so. Joe?" Ethan glanced over his shoulder.

"Her husband is definitely deceased. I checked for a pulse. Yeah, I think we should make her as comfortable as we can. It's getting ready to rain and she's lying in a ditch." Together, he and Ethan carefully moved her to the middle bench seat of the van.

I wet a rag and wiped as much of the dirt from Maryann's face as I could. She groaned a couple of times, but didn't open her eyes. "Maryann?" I hated to disturb her, but wanted to ask a few questions. What person in their right mind would speed on these roads?

"Bruce?" Her eyelids fluttered then opened. Panicked, she slapped at my hands and struggled to sit up. "Where's Bruce?"

"He's by the car." I couldn't tell her he was dead, I couldn't. "What happened?" I waved Joe over.

"We were coming around a curve and the car sped up. Bruce tried to slow down, but he said the brakes weren't working." She put a hand to her head. "Oh, my head hurts. Where's Bruce?"

Tears sprang to my eyes as Joe took her hand in his and crouched beside her. "We've called the ambulance to help you, Mrs. Franklin. I'm…I'm afraid Bruce didn't make it."

Her cry ripped at my heart. Right along with the notion that our Maui killer had claimed another victim. What were the chances that a rental car's brakes would fail? I mean, they kept these cars in mint condition. No, with the other things that had happened recently, I felt pretty certain that someone had wanted the Franklins dead.

I stood and leaned against the car. That 'someone' was ticking down a list, at least it seemed like to me, making the deaths look like an accident. A list! I remembered the cigar box. I needed to check it as soon as we returned to our room. Something told me my procrastination could have let a clue go by undiscovered.

19

Sunburned, exhausted, and with a camera brimming with pictures of the most beautiful scenery, I plopped on the bed and stared at Mrs. Aldrich's box. What I really wanted to do was set aside anything that had to do with the mystery and enjoy what was left of my honeymoon. Obviously, that wasn't going to happen.

Against the backdrop of Ethan's tuneless singing in the shower, I slowly opened the lid of the box and peered in. A few sheets of paper and a couple of photographs were inside.

I lifted a photograph and studied the beach it depicted. Two men, their faces in shadow, stood beside the water. From their body language, it was obvious they fought about something. The next picture was taken through a window where a man, his back to the camera, riffled through a dresser drawer. A dark smudge on his upper arm disappeared under the sleeve of his tee shirt. Yes, Mrs. Aldrich had done some snooping, but her photography skills left a lot to be desired.

After returning the photos, I pulled out the paper. Every current guest residing at the Wahine Bed and

Breakfast was listed. Mr. Jamison's name was crossed off. The Wahine's were also listed, with stars beside their names. Did the stars mean Mrs. Aldrich suspected them, or did it mean she thought they were in the clear? Instead of giving me answers, her notes raised more questions.

Ugh. I fell backward, banging my head on the headboard. That's what I deserved for my momentary temper tantrum.

Ethan stepped out of the bathroom, a towel wrapped low on his hips, while he scrubbed at his head with another towel. "What's wrong?"

"I looked at Mrs. Aldrich's notes, such as they are." I moved the box closer to him by using my foot.

"That's the beach right outside." He pulled out a photo.

"Are you sure?"

"Pretty sure." He picked up the other picture. "And this is Mr. Jamison's room, I think. They all kind of look the same."

I snatched the pictures from his hand. "You're right. Why didn't I see it? Any idea who the guys are?"

He shrugged. "Not a clue."

I scooted to a sitting position and hugged a pillow. "I need to ask some pointed questions at supper. Speaking of which, I need to get showered and dressed."

"You look beat." Ethan glanced at the clock. "Why don't you rest, and I'll order in. You can ask questions in the morning."

I took his advice and snuggled down. When I woke, the sun had fully set. Wondering what Ethan had done to occupy himself, I grabbed a clean set of comfie clothes and went to take my shower. By the time I was finished, murmuring voices drifted from the living area. One glance at the bed showed the cigar box missing. I moved to the living area where my family huddled around the coffee table and box.

"This is definitely right out your window, but the angle doesn't come from in here." Joe tapped the photo against his leg then moved to the arcadia door. "I'd say the photographer hid in those bushes."

"What do you think the man was looking for in Jamison's room?" I sat next to Ethan.

"It isn't Jamison's room." He turned and stood beside me to point at the other photo. "It's the Aldrich's, I think. Unless Jamison wore lipstick."

Sure enough, a tube of peach, the same shade Mrs. Aldrich used to wear, was lying on the dresser. I studied the photo closer. In the corner, a floral fabric hung out of the closet. She'd taken a photo of her killer!

"My name's on that list." Uncle Roy crossed his arms. "I'd like to see some low-life snake come sniffing around here."

"I want you taking precautions, Roy." Joe shook his head. "This isn't funny. Nobody at this hotel is safe until this murderer is caught. I need to have a serious talk with Manano. Summer, I'm taking these photos with me."

"Not until I make copies." I grabbed the box and its contents. "I made a promise to Mr. Aldrich, and I intend to keep it. I'm going to the business center."

"Not alone, you're not." Ethan stood and grabbed the card key to our room. "Joe, we'll bring these by your room when we're done."

"Sounds good."

We left as a group, the other four going to their cottage, while Ethan and I headed to the main building. The business center was a fancy name for a closet of a room that housed one computer and a printer that also acted as a fax and copier. Black and white, but at least we'd still have the jest of what was on the photos.

Ethan waited patiently while I made the copies, then took my arm to walk me to Joe's room. I wanted to ask what when on in his handsome head, but decided Ethan needed a few minutes to work through something. I was torn between wishing he'd take me back home to Arkansas or stay in Hawaii to finish what someone else started.

We left the building and took the long way to Joe's cottage. The path that led along the beach. I slipped my hand into Ethan's, and he gave it a gentle squeeze.

"Want to take a moment to watch the waves?"

I nodded. "I'd love to. There hasn't been a lot of romance on this honeymoon, has there?"

"No, and we need to remedy that." He led me to a small rise in the sand.

We sat, his arm around my shoulder, my head on his chest, and watched the waves caress the beach. God often outdid himself with his creation, and the view ahead of us gave testimony to that fact.

The moon cast a silver path over dark water. What would it be like to walk that path? Hand-in-hand with Ethan, just to discover where such a heavenly path would go. I sighed and snuggled deeper. Ethan kissed the top of my head. We'd definitely have to come back and have a proper honeymoon.

"Shhh." Ethan straightened.

Closer to the water, a man walked, head down, scraping his feet through the wet sand. He stopped and peered across the ocean waves.

"That looks like the same profile in Mrs. Aldrich's photo." I tried to peer at him in the dark, to no avail. "Should we say something to him?"

"No." Ethan stood slowly and pulled me behind a hibiscus bush. "Just watch. Maybe we can follow."

The man seemed deep in thought, hands shoved into the pockets of his shorts. From his slim build, I guessed he might be a young man. A native, even. If my guess was correct, it would lower the suspect pool. I shook my head. We didn't even know whether the young man was up to no good, and here I was jumping to conclusions, as usual.

After several minutes, he strolled a few yards farther down the beach and plopped onto an old sofa someone had left under a palm tree. I'd always figured it belonged to a vagrant, but maybe not. Maybe it was a cheap way for people to enjoy the view.

"Has it occurred to you," I said, tugging on Ethan's arm to get his attention. "That most of our time on this beach has been to spy on people?" I'd rather be curled up in a beach chair or snorkeling.

He chuckled. "So, it has. Look, he's moving again, and he just lit a cigarette. Do any of the guests smoke?"

"I don't know, and I'm sure if the staff does, they aren't allowed to do it out in the open." I sighed. I'd created a monster when I roped Ethan into helping me solve the last two mysteries I'd gotten involved in. He said it was to keep me safe, but sometimes I wondered. I allowed him to drag me until the man disappeared out of sight among the buildings of the B & B.

"We've lost him." Ethan's shoulders sagged. "Might as well go to Joe's."

"You're enjoying this, aren't you?"

"More than I should." He gave me a hug. "Just think, most people on their honeymoon spends all their time in their room. We're seeing the whole island by chasing these clues."

"Imagine that."

"Feeling neglected?"

"A little." I forced a smile. "Why is it that everywhere I go, someone dies?"

"Just lucky, I guess." He slid his hand down my arm and took my hand. "Come on. I'll love you until your blood boils after we drop these off at Joe's."

"Promises, promises." Of course, just the thought of his promise put a spring in my step.

Instead of knocking on Joe's cottage, Ethan pushed open the door and entered as if he lived there. I shrugged. Since Joe and April weren't married and shared the cottage with Uncle Roy and Aunt Eunice, things were safe, or they'd better be. If Joe tried anything with April, officer of the law or not, Ethan would skin him alive. I grinned. I might pay to see that.

"About time." Joe uncurled from the sofa. "Everyone else is already in bed."

"Wish we were." I clapped a hand over my mouth.

Ethan gave me a warning look. "We were following someone we thought looked like the guy in the photos. But we lost him." He handed Joe the papers, folding and tucking our own copies before stuffing them into the back pocket of his jeans.

"I'll meet with Manano tomorrow and let you know what he says." Joe set the photos under a crystal vase.

"If he's a crooked cop," I stated. "You're putting yourself in danger."

"Nothing new." He narrowed his eyes. "Or should I say nothing more than what you do to me."

"You're a regular comedian." I crossed my arms. I loved my cousin dearly, but must he always be such a thorn in my side?

"You two act like brother and sister." Ethan took my hand and led me to the door. "See you at breakfast, Joe."

Breakfast! My own opportunity to ask questions. Why did I always take it as a personal challenge to solve a crime before Joe, who was much more qualified? We'd been in some form of competition our entire lives. Time to get over it.

"Do you really think Manano is going to cooperate?" I asked.

"No, I don't. The man's mixed up somehow, I just don't know how."

A strange hissing flew past us, then the sound of a soft thunk. "What was that?" I whirled, trying to see in the glow of the moon and scattered decorative lighting.

Ethan peered at the wall behind us. "A dart. The kind that comes from a blow gun." He straightened and grabbed my arm. "Let's..."

A sharp pain stabbed my thigh. Literally. I glanced down at a three inch dart sticking out of my leg. "I've been shot!" Mercy! My legs buckled.

Ethan hefted me in his arms and dashed back toward Joe's cottage. He grunted and stumbled, but kept going.

Since we'd left, Joe had locked the door. Without setting me down, Ethan kicked at the door until Joe answered, dressed only in a pair of cotton shorts.

"What?" One look at our faces and me in Ethan's arms must have answered his question. He opened the door to let us in then slammed and locked it again.

Ethan sat me on the sofa and lifted the leg of my pants. "I don't know if we should pull it out or not."

"What if it's poisonous?" I bolted up. "Yank it out."

Joe bent, then straightened with another dart in his hand. "This was in the back of Ethan's calf." He held it up to his nose and sniffed. "I don't detect an odor."

"Another warning?" Ethan pulled the one from my leg.

I hissed. "Someone shot you, too?" Oh, wait until I got my hands on that someone. I was used to getting shot at, unfortunately, but took personal offense when the target was someone I loved.

A rock shattered the window. I screamed and dove under the coffee table.

Joe picked up the rock and read what was on the paper wrapped around it. "Go home." He sighed. "Guess I'm going to start wearing my gun."

20

My leg didn't hurt too much the next morning, but I was tempted to stay in bed and pout anyway. Ethan was too worked up over our recent attack to make good on his promise to love me into oblivion. Instead, I showered and changed into a sundress, ready to take on a table full of suspects, I hoped. Most people couldn't turn down a full made-to-order breakfast, and most mornings were no exception.

When we entered the dining room, I glanced around before sitting at the table with the rest of my family. True to his word, Joe's service revolver was in its holster around his shoulder. I wondered whether it was legal for him to carry it like that while not on duty, but wasn't about to ask.

The Wahines sat around one, the rest of the guests scattered among the other tables, not that there were many of us left. Maybe that accounted for the frown on our robust host's face.

David Hatcher fit the body build of last night's beach wanderer, so did Leroy Wahine and the gardener, Manuel Mokiao. Of course, that didn't necessarily mean our attacker was a man. I was sure most Hawaiian women could blow a dart, or was that stereo typing? And, if the darts were poisonous, we'd be dead by now. Ugh. My mind was wandering, again. I needed a concrete clue to follow.

"Joe, can I go with you to talk to Manano?" I stabbed my fork into a chunk of pineapple.

"No." He downed the rest of his coffee and stood. "I don't think he likes you."

"That's never stopped her before," Uncle Roy joked.

"Ha ha." I folded my arms and dropped my head on them. "I haven't a clue, literally. I'm going to the bathroom."

Wanting to be alone, I shook my head when April made a move to follow. I needed to do something, and it wasn't the restroom. Instead, I ducked out the back of the main building. If one of their employees smoked, there'd be an ash tray. There was, and a few of the butts had lipstick on them. Still, the person on the beach last night had been a man, I was certain. So, tonight, I'd come back and find out who smoked. Then, I'd pounce on them with questions. I didn't have a lot of faith in Manano. If Joe wanted to do things the proper way, well, good for him.

Instead of returning to the table, I stopped right outside the double doors. Luckily for me, the Wahines' and Susan and David sat close enough for me to eavesdrop. So far, no one was speaking. I rubbed my leg where the dart had pierced me. It didn't hurt, really, not nearly as much as the knowledge that someone would take down Ethan to get to me.

Footsteps alerted me to the fact someone was either leaving or joining one of the tables. I froze and held my breath.

"This is out of control," Susan hissed.

"I know." Manano! "I thought when Jamison was found dead, things would settle down. Instead, they're escalating and I have no idea who's behind it."

"Not that Banning woman?"

"No." Manano scoffed. "I just used her to set the real killer off guard. She's not smart enough to head up an operation like this."

Whatever. I could head up anything.

If Manano had no idea of the killer's identity, and either Susan didn't either or she was a very good actress, I was back to square one. The idea didn't sit well with me. With only a few days left on the island, I needed to get to the bottom of all this. My gut told me it had something to do with Jamison's scam to get people to buy into a timeshare. Obviously, the list from the box was a list of those people.

Except, Uncle Roy wasn't listed. Maybe because he hadn't actually paid any money yet.

Another set of footsteps caused me to stumble backward. I tripped over a planter and landed square on my bottom. Goodness, I was a graceful as a turkey. I stood and rubbed my aching tush.

"Summer, if you're finished goofing around, would you mind stepping inside so Officer Manano and I could have a word in private?" Joe stared, brow furrowed.

"Sure." It didn't take a rocket scientist to know I'd been eavesdropping. Sigh. I started to head back to the dining room and changed direction. I needed some quiet time with the Lord.

A conversation with Him was long overdue. I wanted to smack myself in the head. Like the other times, I plowed forward without asking for His guidance. When I finally did, pieces would start to fall into place. Why should this time be any different?

I popped back to the patio, asked Joe to tell Ethan I was headed to the beach, then hurried off before anyone could stop me. I desperately needed some prayer time alone.

In clear view of our cottage, I plopped into an empty beach chair and watched the sun glimmer on the waves. Outside, in God's creation, was the best place to get close to Him, in my opinion. Walls built by human hands left something out. A bit of God's glory, perhaps.

I bent my knees and pulled the skirt of my dress to cover them. The morning wasn't cold, but a bit of a chilly ocean breeze blew, kissing my face and playing with my hair. Closing my eyes, I lifted my face to the sun.

No words were needed. Just an open heart. God knew my worries, my fears, my needs. I allowed myself to empty in His hands. Soon, the breeze carried more than the salty scent of the water, it held His promise to never leave me. Tears rolled down my cheeks, not sad tears, but ones of happiness. Strange, not how wonderful prayer made me feel, but that I took so long to take the time to worship.

Drying my tears on my knees, I stood and stretched. I turned to see Ethan sitting a few feet behind me. My guardian angel. I should've known he wouldn't let me too far out of his sight. Without speaking, I moved to him and slipped my hand in his.

He kissed me and whispered that he wanted to make good on his promise. I warmed hotter than the volcano and let him lead me to our room.

###

Later, Ethan and I snuggled on our deck and watched Joe trudge toward us. I guessed he finally had some information for us.

He stopped and took an empty deck chair. "Well, Manano is an idiot."

I giggled. "That's no surprise."

"I have no idea how he became a cop." Joe sighed. "I showed him the papers, he took them without looking at them, and then promptly told me that I had no jurisdiction on Hawaii and to stay out of his investigation."

Now, my cousin knew how I felt on a regular basis. "And he promptly told you he has no suspects, am I right?"

"I guess you gathered that much from eavesdropping. The only thing of value he told me was that Susan and David aren't talking about you being a hassle." He narrowed his eyes. "And this goes no farther than this deck. But, rather, they're talking about David's wife."

"His wife?" I straightened.

"Seems she found out about their little affair. They were buying a timeshare so they'd have a safe place to get together. Anyway, Mrs. Hatcher has the ability to ruin Susan's reputation. Seems she'd the daughter of her town's mayor."

Oh, what tangled webs we weave. "We're back at square one."

"Pretty much."

"Except." Ethan spoke up. "We're pretty sure the murderer is a man. We also know Jamison died by poisoned nuts of the same variety the hotel gives out. We also suspect our killer might be a smoker."

"We do know a little." I felt better. "But, we're running out of time. How safe would I be back home if someone really believes I might know their identity?"

Joe shrugged. "No idea. But if we don't find out something soon, we'll have no choice."

"What do the Wahines say about the scam?" Ethan asked.

"Mr. Wahine had no idea there were rumors that he was selling. This patch of island land has been in his family for generations. They're behind on taxes, but he believes he can pull out with a steady stream of customers. He's going to put extra effort into marketing."

"But if someone were afraid of losing the family land, that would be an incentive for murder." I chewed the inside of my lip. "I think we need to focus more on those directly involved with the B & B." It seemed as if all the guests were as much victims as we were. Some, more so, since they'd been killed.

"Manano did confirm that the brake lines were cut on Bruce and Maryann's rental. That makes the body count up to three. Whoever our perp is, he's racking up bodies. I don't want one of us to be next."

Neither did I. "So, what do we do?"

"What if we all choose someone to watch? Roy and Eunice take Mr. and Mrs. Wahine, you and April take the staff, and Summer and I take the Wahine kids?"

"That's a great idea, Ethan." I patted his shoulder. "We're going to solve this. I can feel it. My question, though, is why aren't we threatened in the daylight? Every time we've been attacked, it's been under the cover of night. I think we need to find out when people around here go to bed. If someone constantly sleeps in and then stays up late, they could be at the top of our suspect list."

"Kind of an elementary way of looking at things," Joe stated. "But, it's as good a theory as any other we have."

Well, thank you for the left-handed compliment.

Manuel, the gardener, strolled by with a leaf blower in his hand. He nodded a greeting and turned on the obnoxious tool, scattering leaves and flower petals all over us. "That's rude." I had to shout to be heard.

Ethan put a restraining hand on me. "Don't irritate any of our suspects. We're in enough trouble." He picked a leaf out of my hair.

I crossed my arms and gave Manuel's back an evil glare. It wouldn't do any good to complain to the Wahines. Not with them being our only solid suspects. Of course, if the Wahines wanted us dead, all they had to do was poison our food. "I don't want to eat anymore meals here."

"Okay, Miss Random." Joe stood. "I'm going to go explain our plan to the others. We'll meet at lunch," he glared at me. "Somewhere. And compare notes."

"We'll meet in the dining room." Ethan smiled. "If the food were poisoned, they wouldn't eat it. Just don't eat anything the Wahines don't eat."

Oh, but my husband put too much trust in people.

21

"What do we do now?" Since Ethan and I were assigned the task of shadowing the Wahine siblings, we needed to find out what their morning routine was.

"Camilla works the front desk, not sure what Leroy does." Ethan headed toward the reception area. "I've seen him all over the island."

"We need to split up." And I needed coffee.

"I hate that idea, but you're right. You take Camilla. At least there will be people around."

"But what about you? You were stuck with that dart, too." Ethan needed to stop being a hero. We were both in danger, possibly even the rest of the family, although no attempts had been made to harm them. Yet.

I gave Ethan a kiss, promised to be careful and not tire myself too much not to enjoy the luau scheduled for that evening, then hurried to the foyer of the main building. I grabbed a few tourist brochures and poured a mug of coffee before finding a plush wicker chair to spend some time in. A place where I could watch Camilla work at the front desk.

Luckily for me, the foyer was also a place for

guests to sit and relax. Comfortable seating arrangements were scattered throughout the room, inviting folks to linger, so I wouldn't attract too much attention by sticking around.

The phone rang a couple of times, but other than that, no one stopped by the front desk. How could Camilla stand it? At least back home in the candy shop, I had candy to make in between customers. There was always plenty of work to do. I'd be bored to death otherwise. I was bored now. How many times could a girl read the same travel brochure? I sighed and picked up my mug, now cooled to where I could take sips without scalding myself.

The view outside the floor to ceiling windows was breathtaking. The ocean waves capped with white. A few surfers on colorful boards. Palm trees swaying in a gentle breeze. What I wouldn't give to be outside, hand-in-hand with Ethan.

"May I help you, Mrs. Banning?" Camilla smiled, her mocha face beaming. "You've been here for a while. Are you all right? Do you need something?"

"No, I'm fine. Just enjoying the view." I set my mug back down on the wicker end table. I guess an hour was too long to sit unnoticed.

"Wouldn't the view be easier to see from outside?" Camilla's grin stayed in place. "I'm leaving for lunch and want to make sure there isn't anything I can help you with first."

"No, I'm fine. Trying not to get too much sun." Great. Now, I'd have something to do. I could follow Camilla, incognito, of course. I wondered whether Ethan fared any better.

Leaving the mug on the table, I waited a few seconds for Camilla to leave, then followed her, keeping out of sight behind bushes and posts. She headed for the beach and turned right. There wasn't going to be a lot to hide behind soon. Hopefully, she would be focused enough on her destination not to turn around.

She sped-walked to a cottage, just off the hotel grounds. The little cottage needed paint, but might once have been a nice shade of sea-foam green. Camilla knocked, a man's voice called out for her to go in, and she pushed open the door.

A boyfriend, perhaps? One she didn't want the family to know about, or did I once again jump to conclusions?

Camilla stepped inside, kissed the young man on the lips, then pushed himself with a declaration that someone might see. Definitely not an approved romance. I wondered why. The boy was attractive and looked like a native. Was it possible the Wahines had someone else in mind for their daughter? I shrugged. It wasn't any of my business. There were plenty of other things to take up my time.

Heading back the way we'd come, Camilla caught me watching. I quickly studied the sand as if looking for shells, and meandered toward her.

When I got close, I glanced up. "I took your advice and decided to enjoy the outdoors."

"Uh huh. Were you following me?" She crossed her arms, tapping a bare foot against the sand. "You're a guest here, Mrs. Banning, but that doesn't give you the right to interfere in our personal lives."

"I…" Wanted to lie. But, I couldn't. "I'm sorry. Are you dancing at the luau tonight?"

"Yes." Camilla turned her back to me and started walking. "Leroy and I always participate. It's a tradition that, sadly, might be coming to an end."

"What do you mean?" I half-skipped to catch up with her.

"Nothing."

"It's not a secret that the B & B is hurting for money. After all, that's why Jamison did the scam."

She cast a sideways glance at me. "Really? I had no idea we were in financial straits. You shouldn't listen to gossip, Mrs. Banning." Stopping, she whirled to face me. "My family had nothing to do with Mr. Jamison's death!" All prettiness fled from her face. Spittle escaped her lips. "He was an evil man out to harm innocent people. If you believe the rumors, then you are as bad as he was." With a swish of her flowered skirt, she dashed back to the main building.

That didn't go over very well. I'd managed to make a normally placid-seeming young woman angry enough to spit. I really did have a gift.

A glance at my watch showed it was almost lunch time. Hopefully, the others fared better. Just in case they did, I didn't think it a good idea to discuss things openly in the dining room. I waited outside while they arrived and recommended Uncle Roy's and Joe's cottage since it was larger, and we could talk in private. They all agreed. We hit the buffet and, with plates loaded down, headed toward our meeting.

Once we'd settled into the comfortable chairs and sofas at the large cabin shared by my relatives, I made a motion for prayer. "We seem to be heading into this investigation without asking God for direction. If I've learned anything from the past, it's that not asking Him is a big mistake."

Aunt Eunice patted my knee. "I agree. See, Roy,

we did raise her right."

Was there any doubt? I frowned, wondering, exactly, what her comment meant. Of course they raised me right. If not for their love after my mother's death when I was five, I knew I would have perished. Not once in the last twenty-five years have I ever felt unloved.

We held hands while Uncle Roy prayed. "Heavenly Father, we ask for your guidance. Without it, we're nothing but a bunch of chickens running around. We need to find this killer before he kills one of us. Amen."

Uncle Roy's prayers were nothing if not short and simply stated. We all sat. Joe, the showoff, had notes. Fine, he could take charge. I sat back and folded my hands in my lap.

"Roy, Eunice, what did y'all find out?" Joe poised a pencil above his notebook.

"That the Wahines are boring." Aunt Eunice shook her head. "The Mrs. scurried around like a mouse putting last minute touches on the luau. Mr. Wahine stayed in the library crunching numbers on that old dinosaur-of-a-computer. When I went in on the pretense of looking for something to read, he glared at me the whole time." She huffed. "The man has two personalities. He's like a Dr. Jekyll and Mr. Hyde."

Joe scribbled something on his paper. "Roy?"

"Nothing more than what Eunice said. They don't seem up to much at all."

"Well," Joe flipped a page in his notebook. "The gardener is busy getting the place ready for the luau. Didn't do anything out of the ordinary."

"Neither did the maid," April injected. "But she is

a nervous little thing. Flitted in and out of the pantry several times, counting the boxes of nuts. Almost like she was afraid of a reoccurrence happening on her watch. I think she's clean."

"Leroy did gopher work all day. He checked the pig roasting pit, which smells heavenly." Ethan grinned. "And set up tables and chairs on the beach. But," he held up a finger. "He does smoke. So, he's most likely the man we saw on the beach the other night. I asked him about the use of that old sofa, and he said he dragged it there years ago because he liked to sleep out under the stars."

"Then, he's our killer!" I clapped.

Joe shook his head. "Just because he smokes and resembles the shadowy figure in the photos, doesn't mean he's our guy. Lots of young men on this island resemble that picture."

The air went out of my balloon. "The only thing I learned about Camilla is that she has a temper when cornered and a secret boyfriend."

"Maybe the boyfriend is our killer." April leaned forward. "What did he look like?"

"Like a young, handsome Hawaiian." Tears stung my eyes. "We're no farther than we were this morning." Someone else would die before we caught the murderer.

"Not necessarily. The Wahines are still our top suspects." Joe closed his notebook. "Leroy is our smoker, Camilla has a temper, and the maid acts as guilty as a kid caught filching cookies."

"Are you going to contact Manano?" I asked.

"No." He looked like I'd asked him to jump off a cliff. "He wouldn't do anything anyway, so why share our hard work?"

Yep, my cousin's ego was showing.

"No, we're going to bring this culprit down ourselves." Joe gave a nod to emphasis his point. "This mystery was brought to us. For once, Summer didn't go looking for it and stick her nose where it didn't belong."

"Thanks, I think." I moved to the window. The noon day sun sparkled on the sand and water, making me realize I hadn't swam in two days. I hadn't even put my feet in the water. Now, workers ran back and forth in preparation for the night. Swimming now would be anything but relaxing. "What do y'all want to do for the afternoon? Snorkel? We haven't been up to the nearby resort yet."

"I'm taking a nap," Aunt Eunice declared. "All this sleuthing has me worn out."

"April?"

"How about shopping? I'm still sunburned from yesterday." She glanced at her perfectly tanned arm. Sunburned, ha! With her blond hair, fifteen minutes in the sun left her a beautiful shade of brown. Me, I tended to burn and peel.

"Shopping where?"

"Some flea markets?" April grabbed her purse. "It'll be fun. We can buy muumuus."

Joe groaned. "If you go out, then Ethan and I have to go. We can't let you two go alone."

"Good grief, Joe." April planted fists on her hips. "It's just to a local flea market. I think we're perfectly fine, surrounded by people, if we stay together. It's almost time to head home and we haven't done anything non-touristy. All of our suspects are busy preparing for the luau."

I stood back and watched his face redden.

Clearly, he was as surprised as I was at April's outburst. Usually, she sat in the background, content to be the silent observer. I wanted to cheer.

"It's not a good idea." Joe stepped forward.

April took another step to meet him. "I need some girl time without men shadowing us."

My face hurt from grinning. Ethan gave me a look that said to knock it off. I mouthed, "What?"

"Where are we going to go, Joe?" By now the two stood nose to chin. "We're on an island."

"I'd rather go to the flea market than nap," Aunt Eunice said.

"See, now there're three of us." April crossed her arms.

"There were three stooges, too." Joe shook his head. "I can't force you to stay."

Hmmm. Sure he could. Joe had every intention of following. I glanced at Ethan. Yep. We'd have company for sure. Maybe we could ditch them.

I met April's gaze and knew without saying a word that she had the same idea. We could fill Aunt Eunice in on the plan once we were in the van. I didn't know, or care, what vehicle the guys would drive.

"I'll go put on some comfortable shoes. Meet you at the van in fifteen minutes." I planted a quick kiss on Ethan, then dashed out the door and to our cottage. A Hawaiian flea market ought to be fun. What could possibly happen at one of those?

22

Not the way I envisioned spending my honeymoon, going shopping with the girls, but so far very little seemed like my original dream of a Hawaiian honeymoon. Oh, well. I snatched the keys from April's hand. "I'm driving."

"Have you ever driven a van?" she asked.

"No, have you?" She shook her head.

"I have an idea. Wait here." Aunt Eunice hefted her purse up on her shoulder and marched for the foyer. Minutes later she returned with a set of keys twirling on her index finger. "Anyone fancy a ride in a baby blue convertible?"

"Yes!" I grabbed the keys and raced to the parking lot. The Wahine B & B tended to have everything a guest could desire, why not a car? "Hurry." I wanted to put some space between us and the guys. I glanced down the lot. There the scoundrels sat in a black SUV, grins on all their faces. Ugh.

I pulled a wadded slip of paper out of my purse and dug for a pen. "Find another piece of paper. Aunt Eunice, I know you'll have something in your purse."

"Why?" She rummaged in her shoulder bag.

"I'm going to jot down some random items and

give the list to the guys. We might as well have some fun while they're following us. Kind of like a scavenger hunt. Winner gets a foot massage."

"Excellent! Okay, I've got it. What's on the list?"

I tapped the pen against my lip. "A picture of all three of them in muumuus." If we were going to do this, we might as well be wicked. I knew they wouldn't turn down a challenge. "A picture of Uncle Roy eating poi." He'd never eat something so foreign.

"This will be fun." April laughed. "On our list, it will have to be Aunt Eunice. We've got to keep it fair."

"True. What's that rice thing with the leaf?"

"Musubi." April spelled it.

"They have to bring one back. We need some harder things that won't be readily available at the flea market."

A knock on the side of the car caused me to scream and drop my pen.

"Yes, Ethan?" I fumbled around my feet.

"What's taking you so long?"

"Don't sneak up on me." I straightened. "Since you're going to follow us anyway, we thought we'd make it fun. So, we're coming up with a scavenger list."

"Fun. Hurry up." He trotted back to the guys.

"A plumeria lei." Aunt Eunice leaned on the seat. "I love the smell."

"A snapshot of a painting in Lahaina's art gallery." April wagged her eyebrows up and down. "It'll be harder for the guys to distract the sales guy in order for one of them to take a picture."

"Good one." My pen raced across the paper.

"And if we say to meet back at five o'clock, that gives us four hours."

"Here's a few things we've added." Ethan appeared at my side again. "Let's switch lists."

"What?" No. We had to do the same list or we might not win.

"Fine." He leaned against the door. "We'll combine the two. We'll still win."

"You're on. Step away from the car." The moment he did, I roared from the parking lot and headed toward Lahaina. "What's on the list he gave us?"

"Well, one thing is a barracuda."

"Just three?" I pressed the pedal harder. "Does it say the barracuda has to be alive?"

"Yes to three, and no to being alive. It doesn't specify."

Aunt Eunice clapped us on the shoulders and then settled back in the back seat. "Piece of cake, sweetie pies. That ninety-nine cent store in Lahaina had a stuffed barracuda, and I know just where we can get a fire eater. Those boys think they can get one up on us, well they've got another thing coming. I'll even be glad to eat the poi, if it means beating them."

We had this game in the bag. One glance in the rearview mirror showed Ethan driving the SUV and gaining ground on us. Were they going to follow and then get their items from the same places we did? "April, pull up the GPS on your phone. We've got to lose those three if we want to win."

"Take a right through an apartment complex, then hang another immediate right, then a left. That will take you to a road that runs parallel with this one, and hopefully, have the guys searching the complex for a while."

"You're a genius." I followed her directions. When we made it to the other side of the complex, we stopped behind a school bus. Only on Maui would little girls in sun dresses get off the bus carrying their shoes in their hands. Maybe someday, when Ethan and I retired, we could buy a little place here and spend part of every year under the Hawaiian sky.

I checked my rearview mirror. No sign of the men, which meant we lost them. We whooped and hollered for a minute and drove away as soon as the school bus moved.

My cell phone rang. I had April hand it to me. "Hello?"

"Where are you?"

"On the hunt, silly." I grinned at April.

"Why did you ditch us?"

Uh-oh. Ethan was not happy. "It's part of the game."

"It's dangerous. Tell me where you are, and we'll meet up."

"No." I turned left toward the ocean. "We'll meet at five to declare the winner. I love you, and us three will be fine. I promise. Bye." I hung up and dropped the phone in my lap. "They did intend to follow us for every piece of the game. Ethan's a little upset with me right now."

"It probably is irresponsible." April rested her arm on the frame of the car and closed her eyes. "But Joe hasn't let me out of his sight all week. I was going crazy."

Hmmm. Ethan and I both lived such busy, full lives, him with high school and football, me with the store, that we were more than happy for large chunks of time together. With Joe a cop and April a teacher like her brother, I would have thought they felt the same way about time together.

I smiled, remembering how Joe proposed at the County Fair right after April handed her County Princess crown to her successor. So romantic. Then, we'd been mauled by a man in a guerilla suit a few minutes later. Oh, good times. There were plenty of memories being made this trip, too, and not all of them were ones I wanted to make.

"There's the store." I pulled into the parking lot. "We should start with the hardest thing on the list."

"Let's get the barracuda out of the way, then there's the art gallery across the street. That's two things in ten minutes." Aunt Eunice was already climbing out of the car. She dashed into the store and returned with a rubber barracuda. With a triumphant lift of her arm, she threw it into the back seat. "Art photo, here we come."

Before we entered the gallery, Aunt Eunice lifted my shirt and shoved the camera against my stomach. "I'll cause a distraction. You take the picture. The other day, I saw a beautiful piece of art embedded in the floor."

Perfect. Within seconds, Aunt Eunice dropped her purse, scattering its contents. The sales woman knelt to help her, and I had snapped the photo. The three of us collapsed in giggles against the car.

"It isn't going to be hard, except for the fire eater and the spear," I said, sliding the camera back into my purse.

"No, It won't." Aunt Eunice climbed in the back. "One of the guys who was going to do the luau tonight eats fire, and also has a spear. I know where he lives. Take a right at the next stop sign."

I climbed behind the wheel. "How do you know this?"

"Well," she crossed her arms and leaned back, looking mighty pleased with herself. "I heard him get fired yesterday and offered him my condolences."

"Why was he fired?" I watched her through the rearview mirror.

She shrugged and studied her fingernails. "Not sure, but he was yelling at that Leroy boy. So, with my natural ability for sleuthing, I looked up his address when Mr. Wahine took a bathroom break."

"Really?" My aunt was a genius. But where had Ethan been? He was assigned to watch Leroy. Maybe the young man would answer a couple of questions for us. "So, we have the fire eater and the list of things to find at the flea market. We'll be finished early." Especially since I figured the guys wouldn't even bother with the hunt until they'd located us.

Aunt Eunice directed us to a small white house with red-and-pink-flowered bushes that covered most of the yard. I decided that was the type of little house I wanted to live in someday, when I won the lottery and purchased a home on Maui.

The three of us scooted from the car and hiked the steps to the front door, which was painted a brilliant turquoise. Aunt Eunice pressed the doorbell in three quick motions, then stepped back.

A very tanned young man with inky hair pulled back into a ponytail answered the door. "Oh, it's you, Mrs. Meadows."

Why didn't he look happy to see my aunt?

"Are you here to ask more questions?" He crossed his arms, drawing attention to bulging biceps.

"No, Kevin." Aunt Eunice frowned. "We need you to show up at the Wahine B & B for five minutes at four forty five."

"Why?" He scowled. "I'd rather never step foot there again. Not after the way that weakling son treated me."

"What happened?" I moved beside my aunt. "They seem so nice." Wouldn't it be great if we won the scavenger hunt *and* went back to the hotel with a juicy nugget of information?

He cursed. "Nice? Lady, you're crazy. That is one wacked up family. They're about to go bankrupt, and now that people are dying like flies, well…"

I got the picture. Desperate people took desperate measures. "Why did they fire you?"

"Why not?" He shrugged.

"Weren't you going to dance in the luau?" Aunt Eunice tried to peek around him. "Do you have a spear?"

"Yes, and yes. But I'm not dancing now."

"Why?" This cryptic exchange made me want to pull my hair out. Obviously, this guy didn't volunteer any information unless you asked the right question. "Why were you fired from the luau?"

"Can we see your spear?" Aunt Eunice stood on tiptoe to try seeing in his house. "We need you to bring your spear. You'll be gone before the luau. Oh, and we need you to eat fire."

"What do I get out of showing up?"

"Focus, people." I glanced back to where April sat in the car staring at the ocean through a stand of palm trees. Smart girl.

Aunt Eunice rummaged in her purse. "You show up on time, and I'll pay you twenty dollars. If you're late, you get nothing, 'cause we'll lose our scavenger hunt."

"Why are you no longer dancing!" I practically stomped my foot.

"Touchy, lady, aren't you?" Kevin sighed. "I'm no longer employed because I punched Leroy in the face this morning."

I raised my eyebrows. "Really? Go on."

"Oh, jeez. I punched him in the mouth because he said I was making the moves on his sister. I'm not, though. I'm dating Malia. Anyway, Leroy said they'd be coming into some money soon, and I wasn't good enough for a Wahine to waste time on." Kevin stepped back, one hand on the door handle. "I'll be there at four forty five at your cottage." He closed the door.

"With your spear!" Aunt Eunice called out. "Don't forget that." She turned to me. "That went well, didn't it?" She studied our list. "We have one little problem, though."

"Now what?"

"The list says we have to have a picture of Ethan, Joe, and Roy in muumuus. We didn't say anything about us having to wear them. How are we going to get that picture?"

23

Good point. I think we needed to be found and the most likely place to find inexpensive muumuus was the flea market. "We'll find them before they find us and snap their picture while they're having theirs taken." Besides, I seriously doubted they would get a fire eater with a spear. That was our winning item, and we got a little more feedback into our mystery.

We made it to the flea market with two hours before the end of the scavenger hunt. Hungry, we bought the seaweed wrapped rice and one extra for proof. Next to the food booth were fresh leis, several of which were plumeria, giving off their wonderful sweet scent. We were cranking on our list.

"Poi." Aunt Eunice wrinkled her nose. "Who has to eat it?"

"Oh, no." April glanced at the thick paste. "Uncle Roy does. Another picture we have to sneak. What if he's already eaten his?"

"There's no way my husband is going to eat that." Aunt Eunice took a deep breath. "If I know Roy, he definitely won't try any. I'll eat some, you take my picture, and it should still count. Right?" She ordered a small bowl. "Do I have to use my fingers?"

"Yes." I got the ready camera. "Just one bite. You can do this."

Aunt Eunice dipped her fingers in the paste and swiped her tongue across them as I took her picture. She worked her mouth back and forth, brows lowered. "Hmmm. Not as bad as I thought. Kind of bland."

"Look." April pointed two booths down. "The guys are slipping on muumuus."

"Great. Y'all stay here." I fished the camera from my purse and darted behind the booths. When the guys lined up, ready for an older woman to take their picture, I zoomed in, snapped the shot and ducked back out of sight. I was made for mystery and spy work. Within minutes, I rejoined Aunt Eunice and April.

Arm-in-arm, we headed to the muumuu booth to buy our own for the luau later. I chose one with pink hibiscus flowers printed on a purple background. We pretended not to notice the men until I turned to find my nose planted in Ethan's chest. One glance at his face showed his displeasure.

"Where have you been?" He scowled.

"Finding the items on our list." I smiled as sweetly as I could and planted a kiss on his lips. "How are you doing?"

"Fine." He sighed. "Are you done running around without sufficient guardians?"

"Yes."

"You're finished with your list?"

"Yes."

"Stay here." He darted back to Uncle Roy and Joe. He returned to us within seconds. "We still have a couple of things. Go back to the hotel and stay there."

I winked at April. Nothing made my sweetheart leave as fast as a competition he was in danger of losing. Since we had everything we needed, going back to the hotel to lounge on the beach sounded like a good idea.

"About something pineapple in a drink?" I started heading for the car.

"The Wahines are probably busy with the luau, and the way they're firing staff, we might have to get our own drink." Aunt Eunice bustled past me.

They fired one person. I shook my head.

"You stay at Wahine?" A little Hawaiian woman stepped from behind a booth. "You careful. Bad man."

"Mr. Wahine?" I still couldn't believe that the jovial fellow I knew had a sour side.

She glanced around. "Be careful. Bad things happen. People die."

"I'll be careful. Thank you." Although I knew of the murders, her whispered warning sent chills down my back. Something was rotten in paradise. Everyone seemed to know more than I did, and I was staying at the place, nosing around.

By the time we got back to our rooms to change for the beach, I was in a fine mess. The more I thought about my lack of clues, the more worked up I got. I needed a powwow with my girls. Hopefully, we could find a private spot of sand in which to hatch our plans.

Grabbing my floppy hat, I slipped my feet into sparkly flip-flops and headed to the beach to meet the other two. Aunt Eunice and April already sat, fruit drinks in hand, in chairs by the water's edge. I must have moped longer than I thought.

"I got your drink." April handed me a tall glass with a straw umbrella.

"Thanks." I untied my sarong, accepted the drink, and lowered myself into a vacant chair. The delectable aroma of roasting pig filled the air. "We need to talk."

Aunt Eunice and April exchanged alarmed looks.

"Stop it. It isn't that bad." I took a sip of pineapple heaven. "We need to set up a sting operation."

"I do not like the sound of that," April said.

"I do." Aunt Eunice leaned closer. "Explain, please."

"Good, because you will play a big part, because of Uncle Roy." I thought for a moment, trying to form my idea into a plan that made sense. "Since Uncle Roy came here to look at a timeshare plan, we need the person responsible to think he is seriously considering forking over some money."

"Jamison is dead," April pointed out.

"Thank you, Sherlock." I glared at her. "But he had a partner who isn't. We need to find out who that partner is. So…" I dared her to interrupt again. "We're going to leave a letter, purposely on accident, from Uncle Roy, somewhere in the hotel tonight."

"That's the dumbest idea you've come up with yet." April shook her head. "Anyone can find the letter."

"I'm thinking we let Leroy in on our little secret."

"How and why him?" Aunt Eunice leaned so far toward me, her chair threatened to tip.

"Because I think the youngest Wahine knows

something. We already know he's a hothead, he smokes, he fits the photos we found."

"Ethan is going to have a fit." April crossed her arms. "You're going to get us in trouble, again."

"No, once we know something, we'll tell the guys. We'll be perfectly safe. Shh."

The subject of our conversation strolled by, giving me an entirely new idea. I prayed Aunt Eunice would catch on. "When does Uncle Roy intend to let the man know he has the money?"

"What money?" Aunt Eunice settled her chair back on all its legs. "Oh, that money! He said tonight at the luau."

Good girl. Leroy's steps slowed.

"I don't like the idea." Oh, this was fun. "That's y'all's retirement fund."

"But Maui is the perfect place to retire." Aunt Eunice raised her glass in a toast toward the ocean. "Other than Arkansas, there isn't a prettier place on God's green earth. Too bad Jamison's dead. We know he had a partner in his business, but we aren't sure who that person is." She wiggled her eyebrows.

April huffed.

I widened my eyes, pleading for my aunt to not overdo her acting. "That's a problem. Ethan and I might be interested in purchasing a share, too. April?"

"I want no part of this." She turned on her side and ignored us.

"Some people don't know a good thing when they see it." I grinned at Leroy. "Hello?"

"Ladies." He gave us a nod and continued on his way, glancing once over his shoulder.

I high-fived Aunt Eunice. "Bait is laid, and our

fire eater is strolling this way."

###

"Roy refused to try the poi, and since you say a cigarette lighter doesn't count as a fire eater, then I guess you win." Ethan tossed the list on the table.

"Wasn't it fun, though?" I snuggled under his arm.

He kissed the top of my head. "Yeah, it was, except for us worrying about where you women were."

"You shouldn't worry so much."

"I can't help it. You drive me crazy."

"But you love me."

"Yes, I do." His chest rumbled with his chuckle. "Now, go put on that over-modest muumuu so we can go to the luau. The smell of roasting pig has me hungry."

I jumped up to do as he bid. Soon, we were headed to a Tiki lamp-lit beach where a small stage was erected and tables were decorated in Hawaiian finery. Pineapples filled with tropical flowers adorned the center of tables. Wicker placemats held brightly colored dishes.

What a wonderful last Hurrah. I found it hard to believe our time on the island was almost over. In two days, we would fly home and return to our everyday lives.

We sat and I glanced around the long table, saddened by how the number of guests had shrunk. I supposed that until the killer was found, no one was eager to rent a room at the Wahine Bed and Breakfast. Afterward, maybe the curious would flock to this part of the island. Warmth cruised through me. I didn't know the Wahines, but as a small business

186

owner myself, I liked to help others succeed. Maybe I could save the B & B and catch a killer at the same time.

Our host announced dinner was served and immediately Camilla and Malia began setting plates of pork and vegetables in front of us. My stomach rumbled, reminding me I hadn't eaten anything but the musubi at the flea market. Oh, the smell was divine.

After dinner, we enjoyed a show of hula dancers, in which Camilla participated, and fire twirlers, one of which was Leroy. My, the Wahines were a talented bunch. Knowing that, it confused me as to how they could let their business be on the brink of selling out. I popped a chunk of fresh pineapple in my mouth. I started thinking maybe there was more to the story then any of us knew.

"Stop staring at people." Ethan leaned close and whispered in my ear. His breath tickled the hair at my nape and sent tingles down my spine.

"Have you noticed that Camilla hasn't smiled once tonight? Leroy seems his usual shifty self, but Mr. and Mrs. Wahine's smiles seem forced."

"If your candy store was going under, wouldn't you have to force a smile?" He straightened and took a sip of iced tea.

"Well, sure, but I wouldn't throw a party, either." No, I'd try to come up with a way to make money and save my business. Exactly what seemed to be happening, except I would find an honest way.

"Excuse me." Malia appeared at my elbow. "I believe you dropped your napkin?"

"Thanks." My napkin was still draped across my lap, so I set the one she gave me aside. Something crinkled from its folds. As surreptitiously as I could, I peeked.

A small square of white paper winked at me. I smiled and slid it into my hand. Pretending to scratch my shoulder blade, I slipped the note under the strap of my bra. Yes, ma'am, I was getting good at the spy technique.

A glance at Ethan showed him engrossed in watching the guys dance and twirl fire while wearing grass skirts. To me, that was an accident waiting to happen. Exciting, yes, but dangerous all the same, and not something I would ever try.

I couldn't wait to get somewhere private and read the note. With it crackling against my skin every time I moved, it was bound to distract me all night.

"Why are you so fidgety?" Ethan put a hand on my thigh.

"I need to use the restroom."

He smiled. "You're like a little kid. Hurry up."

I ducked into the restroom of the main building and pulled the note out of my bra. Written in red ink were the words 'Meet me at five a.m. by the old sofa on the beach. Bring your aunt.'

I knew Leroy must have written the note. He was the only one who thought we were interested in a timeshare and wanted a meeting. Leaning back against the toilet tank, I bumped my head on the wall, twice.

How was I going to get to the beach at that hour of the morning *and* bring Aunt Eunice?

24

At four thirty the next morning, after telling Ethan that Aunt Eunice needed to talk to me about something private and urgent, I knocked on my aunt and uncle's cottage door.

A sleepy, very grumpy, Uncle Roy answered. "Do you know what time it is?"

"Yes. I also know you and Aunt Eunice never sleep later than four thirty and are getting ready to have your morning coffee." I tried to peer around him. "Can I talk to her? Privately, please."

"What's wrong? I've never known you to get up this early." He stepped back to let me enter.

"I do. Sometimes. Besides, this is important girl stuff." And time was ticking.

"Eunice, your niece is here."

I grinned. Uncle Roy only called me *her* niece when he was perturbed with me, which fortunately wasn't very often. This time his annoyance was rather cute.

"Summer?" Dressed in sweats, and with her hair in disarray, Aunt Eunice stood up from the table.

"Can I talk to you outside, please?" A glance at my watch confirmed we were running out of time.

Only fifteen minutes remained for us to make our appointment.

"Okay, but I'm bringing my coffee." She grabbed her mug and followed me out. "I don't know what you're thinking, dragging me out this early."

"We'll talk as we walk. Quickly, though." I headed off at a fast pace to the shoreline as flip-flops in sand allowed.

"Slow down. I'm spilling my coffee."

I stopped to face my aunt. "I got a note last night at the luau telling me to have us meet someone at the beach at five a.m. It's almost that time now."

"Who?" Her eyes widened enough I could see the moon's reflection in her pupils.

I shrugged. "They didn't sign it, but Malia is the one who slipped it to me."

"Did you tell anyone we were coming out here?" She gasped. "You didn't! Oh, mercy, we'll be murdered on a tropical beach and washed out to sea."

"Quit exaggerating. You know they would have stopped us." I put my hands on her shoulders. "We're so close to solving this. We can't stop now."

"Oh, Roy is going to kill me." She set her mug on a nearby table, and we quickened our pace to the designated spot with two minutes to spare.

I eyed the filthy sofa and decided to stand. Besides, if our meeting turned dangerous, I needed to be able to run and push Aunt Eunice ahead of me.

A shadowy form moved toward us from the direction of the hotel. I squinted.

Yep, the same figure that walked the beach, smoking, a few nights ago. Our culprit was definitely Leroy. The young man must be smarter than we all thought, to continue with such a large scheme after

Jamison's death. A scheme to take people's money and kill them. My mouth dried up. Leroy killed Jamison, and I was stupid enough to set up a meeting with him.

"All of a sudden, I'm having second thoughts about being here." I clutched my aunt's hand.

"Too late now." She plastered a smile to her face, teeth gleaming. "Hello, Leroy. I had no idea you were behind this timeshare deal."

"I'm not." He shoved his hands in the pockets of his baggie board shorts. "Jamison was. I'm just continuing what he started. Why should I let a good, possibly profitable, deal go to waste?" He lifted his head. "You want in or not?"

"Wait a minute." I held up a hand. "We need a little more information. Like how much does it cost?"

"Ten thousand dollars."

Mercy! With all the original guests added together, they would have made an easy $100,000. I bit my lower lip. "That's a lot of money, and if this was on the up and up, why have us meet you under cover of darkness?"

"My folks don't know about it. I'm trying to save the family farm, I think is what you hillbillies say." He squared his shoulders. "You want in or not? I don't have all day, and I'm starting to think you're out here fishing for information."

"We are fishing for information." Aunt Eunice moved closer to him and sniffed. "Have you been smoking pot? Why else do you think we're here?" She planted her fists on her hips. "I don't intend to hand over that kind of money without a little more knowledge. As it is, I don't like your attitude and will most likely not purchase your timeshare. Hmmph."

She grabbed my arm and pulled me with her, back toward the cottage.

"What are you doing?" My aunt had gone crazy. I glanced back over my shoulder to see Leroy staring. By now, the sun had risen enough that I could see he was anything but happy.

"You wanted a trap laid, it's laid. If Leroy is the killer, he'll be coming after us."

"Gee, thanks." My stomach dropped three feet.

"Don't go anywhere alone and don't eat anything you don't see the Wahines eat, unless you've fixed it yourself."

"You've gone crazy." Who was this person and where was my aunt? "I might get us into tough situations, but I don't stand up and invite the killer to take a shot."

"You know how I get without the proper amount of caffeine." She whirled. "Do you honestly believe that wimp of a young man killed anyone? He could barely look us in the eye."

"He's the only suspect we've got." She was right. I didn't feel as if Leroy was a killer. A swindler maybe, but I didn't think he had the guts to poison anyone or throw an electrical appliance into an old woman's bath. "I need to look at the photos again. Maybe something will jump out at me."

"Better be fast. I heard there's a tropical storm brewing. I've seen enough movies to know that a storm is a perfect backdrop for murder."

I sighed. My aunt definitely had a flair for the dramatic. After making sure she arrived safely at her cottage, I almost ran to mine. Seeing as to how we'd possibly upset Leroy, I wasn't taking any chances being outside before the sun was fully risen.

When I entered our rented hut, Ethan sat at the small dinette table, nursing a mug of coffee. "Everything okay with Eunice?"

"Yeah." I moved toward the bathroom.

"Well?" Ethan followed me. "Aren't you going to tell me what was so important you had to leave at four thirty?"

I closed my eyes, keeping my back to him. I couldn't lie any longer. "Last night, Malia handed me a note telling me and Aunt Eunice to meet Leroy by the old sofa on the beach." I took a deep breath and turned. Ethan's eyes smoldered. "So, I dragged her out with me. His scam costs $10,000, and we determined he might be keeping the scam going, but that he isn't the killer."

"How did you determine that?" The cold tone of his voice chilled me.

"He's a wimp that won't meet your eyes when talking to you." I squeezed past him to plop on the sofa. "Aunt Eunice came to the same conclusion. Leroy doesn't seem the murdering type."

"You've been wrong before."

Many times, unfortunately. "But, we've laid a trap we're hoping the real killer will fall into."

Ethan ran his hands through his hair. "I'm not going to get angry. I've told you I would help you solve this, but I can't if you sneak off without me."

"The note wasn't to you."

"That's not the right answer." He fell onto the sofa next to me. "You didn't tell me about it because you knew I wouldn't allow you to go."

"True. I'm sorry. If it's any consolation, Aunt Eunice didn't tell Uncle Roy, either."

"Because she chose not to or because she didn't

know about your scheme ahead of time?"

I think he already knew the answer to that question. Ethan put an arm around me and pulled me close to his side. "Do you think you can stay out of trouble for the next three days?"

"I doubt it." My response was given without humor, but Ethan seemed to find it full of jokes.

His shout of laughter almost burst my eardrum.

"I'm being serious. Trouble follows me wherever I go." Sometimes I looked for it, but that was neither here nor there. This particular mystery I did *not* go looking for out of curiosity, a misguided sense of righteousness, or the need to right a wrong. I literally happened to be in the wrong place.

"I wonder if I could find a bumper sticker that says Trouble is Coming?" Ethan laughed harder when I slugged him in his bicep.

A shadow passed the window. I started to jump up to answer the door, but Ethan pulled me back, saying he'd greet our visitor. Okay. Instead, I sat on the edge of the sofa and craned my neck.

Before the person could knock, Ethan had the door open, allowing Camilla to enter. The girl's stony face swiveled my way. Didn't she ever smile? I tried to remember if I'd ever seen her do anything but the pasted-on grin required by employees. Nope. Nothing.

"There is a tropical storm coming." Instead of beautifully lilted words, she spoke like an automaton. "They are not common for this time of year, but my father insists all guests be either in their cabins or in the main building." She gave a single nod. "For their own safety, of course."

Not once had her gaze left mine. Well, she wasn't

the first person not to like me for reasons I couldn't understand. Most likely, once we left the island, I'd never see her or any member of her family again.

I slouched back. If we were to stay inside, how would Leroy be able to make his next move? Or, wait! What if staying in our cabin was the worst-case scenario and would fit in with the killer's plans?

"Thank you." Ethan let Camilla out, taking the chill from the room and returning the temperature to tropical. "I can see the wheels spinning in your head."

"They are." I skooched against the sofa arm and hugged a throw pillow. "I know that the killer couldn't make a storm happen on purpose, but what if he takes advantage of the situation? We're all separated into our individual places. I think we should gather at the larger cabin, or in the main building. Safety in numbers, and all that."

"Hard to take you seriously when you left without those so-called numbers this morning." Ethan pulled the window shutters closed. "Wind is starting to pick up."

"Can't be any worse than a tornado." My gut clenched. "Except we have shelters back home. Where do we go to get away from a tropical storm?"

"Camilla said it wasn't a bad one, just some wind and heavy rain. We'll be fine." Ethan grabbed his room key. "But just in case, I like your idea about us staying with the rest of your family."

One peek out the shutters told me we'd be soaked by the time we arrived. An umbrella was propped in the corner, but with the wind velocity, it'd be next to useless. I sighed. No help for it, we'd have to get wet. I hoped my family had plenty of towels.

196

25

The wind buffeted us, stinging us with rain. Ethan kept a tight grip on my hand, most likely fearful I'd blow away. If this was a small tropical storm, I hated to see what a bad one was.

Aunt Eunice must have been watching from the window because she had the door open the moment we reached for the handle. "Heavens, y'all are soaked." She handed us each a towel.

"I'm guessing you guys were told to stay inside, too?" I dried my arms then wrapped the towel around my head.

"The whole island's most likely battened down," Uncle Roy said. "Only wrench in the plan is staying here instead of investigating this mystery further." He narrowed his eyes. "Yeah, your Aunt Eunice told me all about it, and I am not happy."

"I'm sorry." I really was, but we were headed home soon and I wanted this to be over.

Uncle Roy handed me a steaming mug of coffee. I accepted and breathed deeply of the aroma. Who said I had to solve this mystery? I'd never see these people again, other than my family members. It wasn't the same as a crime committed in my small hometown. Mr. Jamison's murder had nothing to do with me or mine.

I sat in an easy chair, closed my eyes, and

reclined against the back of the chair while keeping my chilled fingers around the warm mug. Except for Uncle Roy expressing interest in something that turned out to be a scam, we could walk away free and clear. *God, is that what you're telling me to do? Walk away? Shove my curiosity into a box?*

Fairly certain He was, a feeling like a blanket of peace settled around me, I sat up and opened my eyes. "I'm no longer going to worry about this latest mystery."

Five pairs of eyes swiveled my direction. "Really?" Joe asked. "Because I wanted to take a longer look at those photos."

Maybe I heard God wrong? I couldn't have. I was pretty certain He didn't want me meddling any longer. But Joe was a police officer. If I detected anything, I could hand it over to him and still stay out of the actual case, right?

"Okay." I wiggled my fingers. "Let me see the pictures again."

Joe grinned. "I knew she couldn't resist." He handed them over. "You may be a meddlesome cousin, but I have to admit you often see things others miss."

"Why, thank you, I think." Compliments from Joe always made me suspicious. Most of the time he was aggravated with me, rather than pleased.

Ethan sat next to me. The faint scent of his cologne and the stronger one of rain and salt air filled my senses. Maybe we should have stayed in our own cottage.

"That's a woman." Aunt Eunice bent over, crowding her head between Ethan and me.

"How do you know?" I asked, peering closer. The

person in the photo wore tropical shorts and a tank top.

"The shape of the rear end, for one." Aunt Eunice tapped her index finger on the picture. "And there's a faint bra strap line through the tank top. She's good. Almost good enough to pass for a guy, if that's what she wanted to do."

"Aunt Eunice, you're a genius!" I kissed her cheek. "That's why we haven't solved this thing. We've been looking for a man." I switched my gaze to Joe. "It's got to be either Malia or Camilla."

"I agree." Joe peered out into the storm. "I think we should take our findings to Manano. I saw him go into the big house right before you two showed up."

"Spending more time with Susan, no doubt." Aunt Eunice grabbed a rain slicker. She really did think of everything when she packed. "If you go, we all go. There isn't a one of us going to stay behind so some evil woman can knock us off."

"I agree." Joe grabbed a lightweight jacket. "We all go. I'll be the one to speak with Mr. Wahine. The rest of you can hang out in the dining room."

"Yes, boss." I gave him a sarcastic salute, in no desire to head back out into the rain and wind. I shivered.

Ethan gathered me close. "We've got a little time for Summer to warm up, don't we? Before we have to head back out?"

"What's the point in drying out, just to get wet again?" Aunt Eunice shook her head. "Go now, and dry off when you're done."

"Here." April handed me a sweater. "It's not a raincoat, but if you tuck it under your shirt, it might be warm enough to put on after we get inside."

"You're the best!" I stuffed the sweater under my tee shirt and giggled, envisioning myself four months pregnant. Ethan must have thought the same thing, because he lowered his head and gave me a kiss that was a little too hot for onlookers.

Face flaming, I turned back to the crowd. "I'm ready to go now."

"I'm sure you are," Joe stated. "The rain will most likely sizzle and shoot off steam when it hits the two of you." He shook his head and led the way outside.

April grinned and followed. I knew she was thinking of a way to get Joe to give her a kiss. My aunt and uncle bustled out next, leaving me and Ethan in the back. Ethan grabbed my hand and we dashed outside.

We splashed through puddles and covered our faces with our arms in a vain attempt to keep the rain out of our eyes. Ethan pulled me under his arm like a mother chicken might cover its chick. It helped keep me dry a bit, but definitely slowed us down. I feared the sweater would be too wet to wear. We should have let Joe go without us and stayed in the warm cottage.

Finally, the main building loomed in front of us like a sanctuary. Ethan shoved open the door. We stood in the foyer and dripped until Malia rushed toward us with her arm full of towels.

"Bless you." I took one and smiled while studying her face. I couldn't convince myself that someone so sweet-looking could be a killer, but she had had the best access to the nuts and to Jamison's room, not to mention the Aldrich's. The cut brake line on the Franklin's car did slow down my thoughts a bit, though. I tended to believe that if a woman was the killer, she had a special friend to do her dirty work.

The dining room held the Wahine family, along with mine. From the scowl on Joe's face, he'd been unsuccessful at his attempt to have a private conversation with Manano, who sat at a table across from Susan, a sappy smile on his face. Seriously, the man needed to get a grip. If he paid attention to half of the things that went on around him, he would know Susan and David are having a 'thing'. The poor blind cop didn't stand a chance.

"What's so funny?" Ethan handed the towel back to Malia, who trailed us like we'd hired her personally, then placed his warm hand on the small of my back and led me to the large table where the rest of the family sat.

"Manano. He's grasping at the proverbial fruit, except someone coated it with olive oil." I reached for the nearby coffee pot, blessing whoever left it on the table for us. Soon, I had my trembling hands wrapped around a hot mug. Since when did it get chilly in Hawaii? Oh, the sweater? I pulled the slightly damp wool from under my shirt and draped it over my shoulders.

"Why don't you go up to the table and tell Manano you want to talk to him?" I asked Joe.

"I did. He said he was busy."

"What about Mr. Wahine?"

Joe shrugged. "I guess talking to him is better than wasting time here, except now I'm nestled in with my girl." He grinned at April. "The way the storm sounds, no one is going anywhere anytime soon. I'll tell him what you discovered later."

What I discovered? Wasn't it a joint effort? Aunt

Eunice is the one who caught on to the person in the pictures being a woman. Why didn't Joe just put a target on my back?

The Wahine siblings strolled past the table, both sets of dark eyes fixated on me. Joe's words probably had more effect on drawing them out than the clandestine meeting on the beach. Right as they passed the table, Malia dropped a tray of plates. I shrieked and almost dove under the table, certain my end had come. Instead, I half-rose in my chair. The gardener, Manuel, scowled and left the room.

All four of them had seemed to listen intently as I questioned Joe. I placed a hand over my speeding heart and took a deep breath. Suspicious or not, it didn't make a lot of sense. What would Manuel have to gain by killing the guests? He'd be out of a job. Same with Malia. If the place were sold, the Wahines would lose their family home. They were on the top of my suspect list. Now, to get the authorities, namely one enamored police officer, to pay attention to what was going on before someone else got killed.

First cup of coffee down, I started on the next and watched the storm blow outside the picture window. What a ferocious beast. Still, the inactivity of sitting made me anxious. But, I'd promised God, sort of, that I would stay out of the investigation and let Joe handle things. Which meant, no matter how tempted I was, that I could not talk to Leroy anymore about his scam.

Instead, I chose to watch every move Leroy and his sister made as they filled drinks, fetched plates of fruits, vegetables, and cheese, argued softly with their parents. How I wished I was a fly on the wall next to their table.

Mr. and Mrs. Wahine looked nervous. Leroy looked like a kid caught with his hand in the cookie jar. Camilla stayed to her sullen self.

I glanced back to the window. A lawn chair blew across the patio. I shuddered, wishing for my storm shelter back home. Did Hawaii get tornadoes? I'd have to look that up someday. Gracious, I was bored.

Rain continued to fall in torrents and had found a leak. Water streamed down the inside of the window.

Malia shrieked and dashed from the room, presumably to get towels. I jumped up to help. Anything to get the blood pumping. If I sat any longer, rigor mortis would settle in.

I skidded to a halt in the hallway. The back door swung back and forth as the storm soaked the wood floor. Bracing myself against the chill, I moved forward and fought against the wind to close it, which amounted pretty much to a soaked petite woman battling a ferocious giant.

Camilla hurried toward me. Wonderful. I could use some help.

With a grin as evil as the Queen of Hearts when she wanted Alice's head, Camilla two-hand shoved me outside then slammed the door behind us.

26

"You are one nosey woman." She had to raise her voice for me to hear over the storm, but the gun in her hand spoke silent volumes. She motioned for me to walk ahead of her. "Keep going until I tell you to stop."

I've had guns pointed at me before. I knew not to do anything stupid. Head down, shoulders hunched, I battled the storm and headed toward a small shack on the perimeter of the property. Did she plan on hiding me until Ethan left? That wouldn't work in any shape or form. My entire family would search the entire island until they found me. Dead or alive.

Escape would be sweet, but I couldn't outrun a bullet. There had to be something I could use as self-defense. Usually, I talked until the killer wanted to shoot themselves, but they wouldn't work when we had to yell to hear each other. By the time we reached the shack, it might be too late.

I glanced over my shoulder, hoping, praying Ethan or Joe, or I'd settle for Manano, were rushing up behind us. Nobody, other than a grimly marching Camilla. How could such a pretty girl be evil enough to murder people? What could possibly drive her to do that? I mean, she lived on Maui!

"Inside." Camilla jabbed me in the back with her gun, forcing me inside an 8 x 10 storage room.

I immediately scanned the area closest to me for a weapon. Even a table leg would work. Anything to set her back long enough for me to flee.

She stood in the doorway, the wind and rain lashing at her back. Why wasn't she moving? It was almost as if she were trying to figure out what to do with me. Maybe she'd acted on the spur of the moment when kidnapping me. Was that a good thing or a bad thing, to take an opportunity without thinking?

"You have no idea what to do with me, do you?" I crushed my arms in a vain attempt to warm myself.

"Shut up." Camilla scratched her head with the barrel of her pistol. Too bad it didn't go off.

"You know, God isn't going to be happy with you when you stand before Him?"

She pointed the gun back at me. "Don't give me your psychoanalytic babble. I'm a Buddhist."

"Oh, well, okay." I chewed the inside of my cheek for a moment. "Isn't Buddha a pacifist?" Is that a word?

"I said to shut up!"

Okay, there isn't anything much worse than a slightly psychotic killer that is growing angrier by the second. I clamped my lips closed and continued my search for a weapon while trying to look like a frightened captive. Well, I *was* a captive, and I *was* frightened, but I didn't want Camilla to know there was fight in me despite that fear. She might shoot me where I stood. I much preferred her confused.

Camilla turned on an overhead light then closed

the shack door. Her wide eyes and frantic pacing scared me more than the gun. The girl was definitely off her rocker. Back and forth, mumbling. I shivered and continued my search, made much easier than the light and the fact that everything was in boxes. *Lord, help me.*

The storm seemed to be abating, which meant my family would come searching, if they hadn't already. Once Malia showed up in the dining room after cleaning up the water in the hall, they might think I'd gone to the restroom. But even that didn't take this long. I refused to have one of my family members shot and killed on my account.

God smiled on me as Camilla turned and opened the door. She glanced out, and I barreled into her, knocking her and the gun to the ground. Without stopping, I dashed through the slow falling rain back to the main building. Camilla's mad shrieks followed, spurring me faster.

I reached for the back door. A bullet smashed into the frame by my head. I gasped and wrenched the door open. Without a backward glance, I raced into the dining room and smack into Ethan's chest.

He held me back at arm's length. "What's wrong? Where have you been?"

I shoved against him. "Get into the dining room and tell Joe to get his gun."

"Summer?"

I pushed harder. "Now!"

Ethan grabbed my arm and we hurried to Joe's side. I took a deep breath and shoved my wet hair out of my eyes. "It's Camilla. She's the killer. She took me to a shack out back and wanted to shoot me."

"My Camilla?" Mr. Wahine stood. "That's

impossible. She's a docile girl."

"Not so much." I plopped into a chair. "Joe, tell me you have your gun."

He pulled aside his tee-shirt, revealing a weapon tucked into the small of his back. "Manano?"

"I'm here. Does Mrs. Banning go anywhere without causing a ruckus?"

A gunshot fired into the ceiling rained plaster on our heads. "Everyone sit down!" A soaked and angry Camilla advanced.

"Princess." Mr. Wahine held his hands up, tears streaming down his face. "What are you doing?"

"Sit down, Dad. I'm doing what you should have done." She waved her gun hand at Leroy. "You, too, you spineless twit."

Mrs. Wahine covered her face with her hands and sobbed. Leroy sat in the chair next to her, his back amazingly stiff for someone without a spine. Camilla maneuvered until she had our group in her sights.

"Your gun, officer." She must have been talking to Manano, because Joe didn't make a move toward his hidden weapon.

"An officer doesn't hand over his weapon." Manano put a hand on the butt of the gun in its holster.

"He does if he doesn't want anyone else to die." Camilla nodded. "Yes, I killed Jamison and Mrs. Aldrich. Had some help with Mr. Franklin, but I guess it's all the same in the eyes of the law. My point is…I won't hesitate to kill again."

Not necessarily true. She hesitated with killing me in the shed. Thank you, Lord. The fact that she'd done so before, might work in our favor.

After Manano reluctantly handed over his

weapon, she ordered everyone to sit. I scooted my chair as close as I could to Ethan and snuggled under his arm. Shivers had my body jerking like someone had stuck me with a live wire. Whether from fear or cold, I wasn't sure. Mrs. Wahine's sobs filled the room, ratcheting my anxiety level to an all new high.

"Leroy, tell Mom and Dad what you did to start all this." Camilla leaned against the doorjamb, reached into her pocket, then pulled out a cigarette. She lit it as if she hadn't a care in the world.

"I've done nothing, compared to you." His back lost all its rigidness as he slumped in his chair.

"Still not man enough to come forward." Camilla blew a smoke ring. "My dear brother, having overheard Mom and Dad talk about the dire financial straits of our childhood home, cooked up a scheme with the late Mr. Jamison, to rob some people of their hard-earned cash. Isn't that right, baby brother?" Without waiting for him to answer, she took another puff on her smoke and spoke while holding her breath.

"Jamison was a fool!" She exhaled sharply. "Threatening to expose everything when Mr. Meadows refused to pay up." She pointed the gun at Uncle Roy.

27

I pushed back my chair and hurried to stand in front of him.

"Get out of the way." Uncle Roy pushed me aside then transferred his attention to Camilla. "If you want to shoot me, little girl, for wanting to know where my money would be going, then go right ahead. I never spend a chunk of dough like that without asking God's direction first. Doesn't mean you can go around killing people."

"I didn't plan to! At first." She dropped the butt and ground it under her flip-flop before lighting another.

"This is about the mortgage?" Mr. Wahine asked. "We're fine, sweetie. Really. Although Leroy's scam was wrong," he glowered at his son. "Filling up the place was a great idea. You killing the folks off…not so much. Probably won't get a single customer now."

"What are you going to do now?" Finally, Joe spoke.

"About what?"

"You can't kill all of us and expect to go free."

"Why not?" She pointed the pistol at him.

I caught my breath and took a step toward my

cousin. Ethan held me back. I frowned at him. Sure, my cousin got on my nerves, but I loved him. I'd take a bullet for any one of my family. I just prayed it would be quick and not hurt too bad. I hated pain.

"Stop doing that," Ethan hissed out the side of his mouth.

"I can't let her shoot them," I whispered back.

"Stop talking!" Camilla's face turned red.

Mrs. Wahine stood, wiped her face on the neckline of her muumuu, and approached her daughter. "You haven't been taking your medicine, have you?" She glanced at us over her shoulder. "She's schizophrenic. Has been since the age of twelve."

Well, that explained a lot.

"What difference does it make?" Camilla's shoulders slumped. "I have to kill everyone and burn the place down."

"Kind of defeats the purpose, doesn't it?" I hadn't meant to say those words out loud.

Camilla transferred her crazy mind to me. "Stop talking. This is all your fault. If you hadn't meddled in things that didn't concern you, you'd be getting on a plane tomorrow none the wiser."

Oh, I was getting on a plane tomorrow. With my family. I couldn't wait to get away from these crazy people. Her stupid remark made me feel a bit like a character in a Scooby Doo episode with those 'meddling kids'.

I sidled up to Joe. "Do something."

"Not yet." He kept his arm around April, who apparently had decided that not speaking might make her invisible.

"Are you waiting for her to shoot someone first?"

"I'm waiting for the cavalry. Stop talking." Joe slowly sat back in his seat.

The what? Everyone was here. I glanced around. Manuel was absent, along with Malia. All we had to do was wait out the crazy woman with the gun. Great. I glanced toward the window, relieved to see the storm had stopped. Why weren't the police here yet?

"What are you looking for?" Camilla marched toward me. "Huh? Hoping for a rescue? Well, that isn't going to happen anytime soon. The road's blocked." She grinned. "I have help, remember? Someone else stands to gain from the insurance money. I'm not worth marrying without money as part of the package." Tears shimmered in her eyes. "Nobody wants a crazy woman for a wife. The insurance money is my last hope."

I shrugged away from Ethan and took a step toward her. Maybe she wouldn't listen to my message of hope, but I had to try. "Everyone has worth, Camilla. You are as precious to God as I am. As your parents. Your brother."

"I told you I'm a Buddhist."

"Didn't he exhibit love?" Oh, why hadn't I studied up on alternate religions for a time like this? Selfish and concerned with my own world, that's why.

"He taught about the true spirituality of the mind. Mine is tainted."

She really had gone off the deep end. Tears burned my eyes. "Well, I don't know anything about him, but I do know how my God feels about you. And He will forgive you. Even for this."

"I'm going to shoot you first." Camilla backed up and lit another cigarette.

I suppose she needed the courage first.

During our conversation, Leroy had circled the room, coming up behind his sister. Ethan and Joe came on each side. With me in front, we surrounded her.

Leroy put a finger to his lips. I nodded and stepped back. Maybe the boy had some guts after all. I did the only thing I could do. I grabbed Aunt Eunice's hands, and we prayed. It didn't take long for Uncle Roy to join us, which was a good thing. My uncle was a prayer warrior of the greatest kind.

The three around Camilla tackled her down.

A shot rang out.

My leg burned for a minute before the pain turned to a raging fire. "I've been hit." My eyes widened, and I fell forward into Uncle Roy's arms.

"Summer's shot!" He laid me on the floor and pressed his strong hands against my thigh. "Eunice, kept praying."

Another shot rang out and someone yelled. I thought it sounded like Leroy, but the pain in my leg overshadowed everything else. I closed my eyes against the tears running down my face. Strange, but the only thing I could think of was that we wouldn't be going home tomorrow.

Sirens wailed.

###

I opened my eyes in the hospital, mortified that I'd fainted over a shot to the leg. All those times I've had a gun aimed at me, I'd never met the bullet.

Ethan slept in a moss green vinyl chair beside the bed, his hand covering mine. Even in sleep, he'd never left me. This I knew without being told.

"Hey, husband."

His eyes popped open and a slow smile spread across his face. "Hey, wife."

"Who else got shot?" My heart lurched at not seeing any of the rest of my family or April.

"Leroy." Ethan shook his head. "He didn't make it. Poor Mr. and Mrs. Wahine lost both of their children yesterday. One to death and the other, most likely, to a mental ward."

"Where is everyone else?" As if my question summoned them, Aunt Eunice and Uncle Roy, along with Joe and April poured into the room. They circled the foot of the bed and grinned like fools. I joined in, my face hurting from the effort. "I want to go home."

"Yes, ma'am." Joe stepped out of the room.

"Will they let me go?" I glanced at Ethan.

"Probably." He leaned over and kissed me. "You've been asleep for two days."

"I have not." What a wimp. A little shot in the leg and I obviously thought I was dying. "I'll have to go in a wheelchair, won't I?"

"Most likely." He cupped my cheek. "But don't worry. I'll push you."

"We thought you were dead." April fell to her knees beside the bed.

I laughed when only her eyes showed over the edge of the mattress. "It'd take more than a bullet in the leg to kill me."

"Obviously." She laid her head against my arm. "You've got a Hawaiian honeymoon you'll remember for the rest of your life."

"And a scar as a momento." I tried to sit up. "Where's my camera?"

"In the suitcase." Ethan laughed. "You took enough pictures for five photo albums."

"Tell me Joe still has the copies from Mrs. Aldrich's box, and the notes. They'll make great keepsakes." I laughed. Happy to be alive, and happy to see my family around me.

Joe arrived minutes later, pushing a wheelchair. "Better get dressed, cousin, because we're busting you out."

"When does our flight leave?" I grabbed Ethan's hand. "Tell me it's soon."

"Tomorrow morning. We've got one night to actually relax on a beach."

"Not at the Wahines." I didn't want to go back there.

Everyone laughed, but sobered quickly. So much heartache. So much death. All because a young woman with a tortured mind didn't understand her value.

Was the young man I'd seen her kiss the one she thought wouldn't marry her without any money? Or was her fear another strike against her illness? My heart ached for the Wahine family, but I wouldn't be searching for answers.

I didn't plan on trying to solve any mysteries for a very long time. I clutched Ethan's hand. No, I was more than ready to start my married life. And, if God was inclined to answer my prayers, I already carried Ethan's child.

I really hoped so.

The End

Be sure to check out the rest of the Summer Meadows Mystery Series:

Fudge-Laced Felonies Book 1
Candy-Coated Secrets
Chocolate-Covered Crime Book 3
Maui Macadamia Madness Book 4

And her new series:
Deadly Neighbors
Advance Notice
The Librarian's Last Chapter

Visit her website at
www.cynthiahickey.com

ABOUT THE AUTHOR

Multi-published author Cynthia Hickey had three cozy mysteries published through Barbour Publishing, with a novella releasing in March 2013. Her first mystery, Fudge-Laced Felonies, won first place in the inspirational category of the Great Expectations contest in 2007. Her third cozy, Chocolate-Covered Crime, received a four-star review from Romantic Times. All three cozies have been re-released as ebooks through the MacGregor Literary Agency, along with a new cozy series. She has several historical romances releasing in 2013 and 2014 through Harlequin's Heartsong Presents. She lives in Arizona with her husband, one of their seven children, two dogs and two cats. She has five grandchildren who keep her busy and tell everyone they know that "Nana is a writer".

www.ingramcontent.com/pod-product-compliance
Lightning Source LLC
Chambersburg PA
CBHW061035120726
47910CB00006B/2264